DEADLY DEEDS

Sara Jane shuddered and took two deep breaths. "I killed him. I killed the other one inside the shack."

Buckskin held her away from him. She nodded. "He was going to shoot you, and I got untied and stabbed him." Her whisper turned into a shriek. "He's dead. Oh, Lord, but it hurts deep down like it's burning on my soul. Blood all over my hand."

She held out her right hand, and Buckskin saw that blood had splattered her fingers.

"You don't have to talk about it. You don't even have to think about it now. It's done. You rest up and you'll feel better. They would have killed us both if they could have. You know that. Something is going on here we don't know about. Now it's my job to find out what it is."

COLT .45 VENGEANCE

37

BUCKSKIN

KIT DALTON

LEISURE BOOKS ⊾ NEW YORK CITY

A LEISURE BOOK®

November 1993

Published by

Dorchester Publishing Co., Inc.
276 Fifth Avenue
New York, NY 10001

Printed in the United States of America.

Chapter One

Lee Buckskin Morgan heard the rifle shots shortly before his dapple gray came to a small ridge. He kicked the mount in the flanks and spurred it to the top of the rise.

Below, a half mile away, he saw a fire billowing up from a barn. Another shed nearby soon would catch the heat and explode into flames. On the small spread, he saw a clapboard house, another shed and a pole corral. Three horses lay dead in the corral, and three mounted riders laughed as they all shot the fourth animal. Then they fired twice into the house and rode off to the west.

Buckskin stared down at the scene and wondered what had happened before he got there. It was too late to chase the raiders who had gunned down the horses. They had a half mile start on him, and his mount was bleary-eyed and had wobbly legs from ten hours of moving across the barren, waterless Arizona mountains.

The only thing he could do was see if the raiders had left anyone alive below. He doubted it, but at least they hadn't burned down the house. That was a good sign.

There was no hurry now. Buckskin stepped down from the gray and led her down the gentle incline toward the house. The shed burst into flames when he was halfway there. What could generate the kind of hate those three men must have had to do this?

Feeling apprehensive, he stepped into the saddle and rode the rest of the way. At the house, he stopped his gray and slid off. As he did, a six-gun barked from the house's open back door, and hot lead whispered over his head.

"Easy, I'm a friend," Buckskin bellowed. "Saw the fire and those three raiders. Wondered if I could help."

No more shots came from the doorway, so Buckskin let the reins to his horse fall to the ground and took a tentative step forward.

"Look, if you don't want any help, I'll gladly have a drink from your well and ride on."

Only silence greeted him. Buckskin took another tentative step toward the door, holding his hands out to the side, well away from the low-tied leather that held his .45 hogleg.

"I don't wish you any harm. Saw those raiders leaving, couldn't do nothing about them. Might be able to help you, if'n you want help."

He waited and watched the doorway. Now he could see a shadow inside the dimly lit interior.

"Yes," the single word came softly but with anger and rage behind it.

"I hear you, ma'am. Just don't shoot. We don't need no shooting. I'm walking toward the door. Aim to help you, if I can."

Buckskin took two or three steps through the Arizona dirt and small rocks and paused, then took three more. He was almost at the door. Just inside stood a woman. She wore half of a tattered blouse that showed tear marks and splatters of blood. One breast was exposed, but she made no move to cover it. Her skirt was torn to the crotch and her left leg showed half of her white thigh. It, too, had blood on it.

He moved gently toward her. Now he could see her eyes, angry and wild, her long brown hair in disarray, an ugly bruise on her cheek, one eye puffy.

"Ma'am, let me help you sit down," Buckskin said. When he stepped toward her, she cowered back, eyes flashing wild with fear.

"I won't touch you, ma'am. Just let me see inside. Is your husband here?"

Buckskin's glance swept over part of the one big room he could see. A man sat tied to a chair; his head had fallen forward, and Buckskin saw the ugly, large exit wound of a bullet. Blood and brains and bone shards were sprayed on the far wall. He frowned and looked back at the woman.

"I'm here to help you. I won't hurt you. Sit down over here."

He moved a chair where she could sit and not look at the man's body. She watched him like a trapped animal, edged sideways and sat on the chair. At once her head came forward; she held it with her hands and began sobbing.

Buckskin checked the rest of the room. It was a starter house, one big room, with a kitchen to the left and a double bed to the right. The bed was rumpled and showed blood spots. He saw heavy cords that had been tied to the headboard and footboard. They had been cut away. She apparently had been spread-eagled on the bed.

Buckskin picked up the chair and the body and carried the deadly load outside, then he returned and removed the cords from the bed. He smoothed out the hand-sewn quilts and set up a wooden chair that had been knocked down.

On the small kitchen table, he found a loaf of bread with one slice cut off it, a tub of butter and a pitcher half-filled with milk. He watched the woman again and saw that she was still sobbing. Best thing for her, get the shock out of her system at least for a while.

He looked at the small cast-iron stove. Buckskin laid a fire, got it burning and went outside to look for more wood. When he came back, the woman had stopped sobbing. She held a big .45 with both hands aimed at his belly.

"No, ma'am, I'm here to help you. I won't hurt you. Never even touch you. Making some coffee for you."

Slowly she lowered the gun, but the hammer was back ready to fire. He walked to the stove, found a battered coffeepot and half-filled it with water from a bucket on the small counter next to the stove. Even if it wasn't fresh water, boiling would take care of any bugs in it. He set it on the stove top.

Buckskin went to the dresser and found a man's shirt. He took it out, unbuttoned it and held it out to the woman. She looked down at her exposed breast, grabbed the garment, quickly pulled it on and buttoned it.

Buckskin went to the counter, wet a hand towel and carried it to her. She looked at it, then took it and nodded. He turned away, letting her clean her face and arms in private.

He boiled the coffee for five minutes, then set it aside to settle. It was a good time to look around outside before it got dark. He figured it was an hour to sunset.

Toward the barn, he found a dead dog of uncertain breed that had been shot twice. The barn still smoked and smoldered. A pile in the corner must have been cut hay for winter feed. A few charred timbers still pointed skyward. The shed beside it had burned to the ground, leaving nothing but charcoal and ashes.

The four horses in the corral were all dead. He looked around but could find no more livestock. Had to be some beef somewhere, but they weren't near the buildings.

He went back inside and found the woman had put on shoes and pinned her skirt together. She sat at the table sipping a cup of coffee.

"Who were they?" he asked.

She shook her head. Her eyes seemed calmer now, but still a twitch spasmed regularly at the corner of her mouth. She watched him with wary eyes and seemed to him ready to leap out of the way at any time. He saw only one of her hands and figured the other still held the six-gun, cocked and ready to fire, deep in the folds of her skirt.

"May I have some of that coffee?" Buckskin asked.

She looked at him steadily, then nodded. He found a cup in the cupboard over the counter and poured one for himself, then retreated to the far side of the kitchen area and tasted it. Not bad.

Buckskin figured the woman had been raped repeatedly, then had to watch her husband tortured and killed. It was enough to cause any woman to lose her mind, yet this ranch wife seemed to have her wits about her, even though she was still in shock.

She might not talk for days or even weeks. He'd seen it happen to survivors after an Indian raid.

"Something Smith," the woman said.

Buckskin turned to her. She watched him.

"Something Smith gang," she said.

"Those were the men who killed your husband?"

She nodded and slowly stood. "Milk the cow," she said.

Buckskin took a step toward her. "I can do that. Where is she?"

"In the barn."

Spur shook his head. "They burned down the barn."

"Horses?"

"Shot four in the corral."

She slumped back to the chair.

"Ma'am, my name is Lee Buckskin Morgan, and I'm on my way to Phoenix. Most folks call me Buckskin."

She looked up at him. "James?"

"Your husband?" She nodded. "I carried him outside."

"Want to see him."

Spur shook his head. "Ma'am, might not be a good thing to do. Tomorrow will be time enough."

"Now." She walked to the door with firm, steady steps. Buckskin marveled at the nerves of steel she must have. She went outside, and he followed. She knelt in the dirt in front of her husband and put both hands on his shoulders.

Tears burst from her eyes again. "I tried, James, I tried. Nothing I could do would stop them. They came to kill you. Know they did. No earthly reason

otherwise. Didn't want me. Must want the land."
She bent forward until her head touched that of
her dead husband's, and she wept again.

After two or three minutes, she stood, wiped her
nose with the sleeve of the shirt and then rubbed
the last tears from her eyes.

"We need to bury him proper," she said.

"Ma'am, that can wait until tomorrow. Getting
dark soon. We couldn't finish."

She frowned, then her brows went up and she
nodded. "Don't call me ma'am. That was my
mother. I'm Sara Jane Nelson. This is my late
husband James. We been here four years getting
this little spread started on this confounded dry
piece of Arizona. Not enough greenery up here to
keep a grasshopper alive."

She led the way back inside. The fire had
burned out. Automatically she went to the stove
and rebuilt a fire, then prepared food. She sliced
bread, poured coffee, took a slab of bacon from
a cupboard and cut off thick slices.

She fried the bacon on the stove in an iron
skillet, never saying a word. When the bacon was
crisp, she forked it onto a kitchen towel to drain,
then dug into a cupboard and took out a small
bottle of brandy.

Without asking she poured a glass for each of
them and handed one to Buckskin.

"Figure I'll need this afore this is all over," Sara
Jane said. "You stay here tonight. Tomorrow we
bury James, then I got me some figuring to do."
She sipped the brandy, then put the bacon on their
plates.

"Not much supper. Tomorrow I'll do better."
She pointed to the Colt in his holster. "You know
how to use that thing?"

"I've fired it now and then, Mrs. Nelson."

"No, call me Sara Jane." She nodded. "Good, glad you can use it. Tomorrow we'll make some plans." She looked up quickly as if she had forgotten something. "Oh, you in a rush to get to Phoenix?"

"No. Just looking for someone there. No hurry."

Sara Jane put the bacon between two slabs of her homemade bread and butter and had a bite. She nodded. "Getting low on bacon and ham, but reckon that won't matter too much now. Got me a new job to do." She looked at him.

"Buckskin Morgan, I figure you seen me at my worst today. Wild and crazy, bawling like an hour-old calf that lost his ma, and me half-naked. Couldn't help it. I'll do better tomorrow. Gets a bit nippy up here at night. You can sleep on the floor, if'n you like. Give you a couple of old blankets for a mattress."

She looked at him hard. "Morgan, you was good to me today. You helped me want to live again, but don't go thinking that you can do me tonight. I got poked enough this afternoon to tear me up some, and I'm sore as all hell. So if'n you be good I won't have to blow your balls off with my .44."

Buckskin chuckled. "Sara Jane, I ain't never taken any goodies that weren't offered first. You have no worries there. I saw those bindings on the bed. I wouldn't mind finding the men who killed your husband and did you that way."

"Tomorrow, Buckskin. We'll talk about it tomorrow. I'm sort of like the chickens, when it gets dark. I like to get to sleep. I heard what you said, but still you remember I got James' old Colt right by my hand. Oh, I always keep the hammer cocked and ready."

"Yes, ma'am," Buckskin said and finished his bacon sandwich. They hadn't lighted a lamp, and dusk closed in quickly. Buckskin went to his horse and brought in his saddle and small carpetbag. When he came back inside, Sara Jane had laid two folded blankets on the floor and put two pillows on top of them. She lay in the bed with the covers up to her chin.

Buckskin figured she hadn't taken off anything but her shoes. He didn't even take off his boots. He just unrolled his blanket, lay down on top of it and the thin mattress of pillows and comforters, rested his head on his saddle and soon went to sleep.

Morning arrived at the same moment two roosters had a crowing contest, and Buckskin blinked and sat up. He wasn't sure of the time, but already Sara Jane had sliced ham cooking in a skillet on the stove, and he smelled already boiled coffee.

"You part Navajo or Chiricahua?" he asked. "You move around here light on your feet."

She nodded. "Figure you need biscuits and brown gravy and some ham to keep you going until noon. By then we'll have had our talk and our work will be done. Then it'll be deciding time."

Buckskin went through the back door, found the outhouse and came back a few minutes later.

The biscuits and gravy were done, and a round of ham was spread out on his plate. The coffee was hot and stronger than he had made.

"Eat up. We got to dig a grave today," Sara Jane said.

They ate in silence. When the food was gone she looked up at him. "James and I knew there was some danger this far from town—the Indians. We had things worked out. No kids for three years, get a good start, expand slowly and pay our way as we went. No borrowing money, not beholden to anyone. Case the Apaches sneaked up on us, we knew what to do. He told me how to shoot myself if I needed to."

She snorted. "Hell, Apaches couldn't be no worse than them damn three white men yesterday. Big one's name is Something Smith, and he's got a ragtag group he calls the Something Smith gang."

"You said something about torture?"

"They pretended to be looking for a hundred dollars in gold we supposedly had hid in the house. No such thing. They beat James fierce, but he couldn't say where the money was, 'cause there wasn't no hundred dollars. Then they shot him in the knee joint, and he hurt something fierce.

"In the end they killed him. When they finished their turns with me I figured they'd burn up the house with me still tied to the damn bed. Surprised me. Smith cut me loose and said he was feeling kindhearted. Said he never had killed a woman and wasn't about to let me be the first.

"Then the bastards laughed, shot our horses and rode off before I could get the gun out of its hiding place. Then you rode up."

She stood. "So, let's dig James a grave. By now I figure we'll have to bury him sitting up 'cause of old rigor mortis doing him stiff as the chair he's tied to."

It took them four hours to scratch out a grave three feet deep. Buckskin used a pick and shovel and still struggled. The ground was like concrete, with rocks and sand that had to be picked apart an inch at a time.

When they finished digging the hole they laid James Nelson in it on his side, stiff and in a sitting position. They wrapped him in a blanket, and Buckskin lowered him in as easily as he could.

Buckskin crawled out of the hole and picked up the shovel, but Sara Jane pushed him away.

"I'm a Nelson and a Kelly and we bury our own dead."

It took her an hour to fill in the hole. They put an outline of rocks around it but had nothing for a marker.

"If things work out, I'll come back with a marker from town," Sara Jane said.

They went back to the house and sat down inside. Buckskin boiled up a pot of coffee, while Sara Jane stared at him. She had combed her hair, washed her face and now took a long breath. She undid her soft brown hair. Now she combed it out, and he saw that it came to her waist.

Her eyes were green, and she studied him again.

"You look like the man who could do the job. I've got a proposition for you. I'm going after Something Smith and his gang. I owe them for what they did to me and for killing James. I need to know how to shoot better. I need some lessons in riding and how to track and trail a man through the desert and how to stay alive in the wastelands. I want you to teach me.

"You do that, Buckskin Morgan, and you can have my body. After I heal up in a week or so, you can fuck me any which way, twice a day until Something Smith is dead. What do you say, Buckskin?"

Chapter Two

Buckskin Morgan almost dropped his cup of coffee. He watched the woman who sat across the table from him. She was serious. He put down the cup slowly.

"Sara Jane, you're saying you want to go after the Something Smith gang and kill them?"

"Exactly. They owe me for what they done to my husband, to me, to our ranch."

"From what you say, they're sadistic killers with a rattlesnake code. How can you hope to find them, let alone kill three outlaws?"

"That's why I need you to help me. I can be tolerable pretty when I fuss all up and try. You want to try me once before you decide and test the waters?"

"No, that's not my point. You're talking about getting yourself killed by these three men. Not a chance that I'll teach you how to shoot just so Something Smith can gun you down. It's out of

16

the question. Forget it. Accept what you have left here, hire a foreman or a cowhand to run your spread, and see what you can make out of the ranch."

"I'll do that, Buckskin, but first those three killers must die by my hand. I'm not hiring you to kill them for me. I want to see the look in their eyes when they know I'm about to send them straight to hell."

As she spoke she unbuttoned the top of her dress. It was cheap calico that stretched tight around her breasts, nipped in at her waist and extended to the floor. Now it had smudges of dirt on it from digging the grave.

She spread back the dress and shrugged it off her shoulders so it fell to her waist. She lifted a thin white chemise over her head and stood in front of him bare-breasted.

"My James liked my titties. Said I had good ones and just the sight of them got him all excited and hard in a flash. You like my titties, Buckskin?"

"Sure do, but I'm not going to touch you. You're still in a state of shock. Don't know what you're doing."

"I know exactly what I'm doing. I'm going to make love with you, and then I'm going to convince you to stay here with me and teach me how to kill and ride and live in the desert. I'm going to fuck you until I convince you to help me."

She moved closer to where he sat, turned his chair around and pushed one of her big breasts into his face. His lips parted, and she smiled as he sucked as much of it into his mouth as he could.

"Now, Buckskin Morgan, tell me you don't like that just a little bit." She gasped as he first nibbled on her nipple, then bit it.

"Lordy, that does get me excited." She pulled her breast from his mouth and knelt between his legs, rubbing at his crotch and finding the start of his erection. She yelped in delight.

"I knew I could get you going. Look at that big fella grow. Oh, glory, but I bet he's a good one." She rubbed his growing hard-on, and it grew and grew. Quickly she worked at the buttons on his fly until they came open and her hand could dive inside.

She parted his underwear and grasped his erection. Slowly she pumped it up and down and watched his expression.

"Yes, I can tell you like it." She worked his erection out of his pants and kissed the purple head. It jerked in anticipation.

"Yes, Buckskin. Right here, right now." She bent and pulled down her underclothes and threw the bloomers on the table. Then she caught Buckskin's hand and tugged him toward her. She pulled him down to the floor, lay on her back and pulled up her skirt.

Already her legs were parted and her knees lifted. She held out her arms to him.

"Please, Buckskin Morgan, love me soft and tender and let me show you how good it can be. Once or twice or three times. I've got three places that I can love you. Right now before you take your pants off and here on the floor."

She caught his erection and pumped it back and forth a dozen times, then fondled his scrotum, tenderly massaging his balls and bringing beads of sweat to Buckskin's forehead.

"No promises," Buckskin said as he went on his knees between her white, tender thighs.

"No promises."

She caught him and pulled him lower, then

angled his hot tool to the right spot, caught his hips and pulled him into her.

Sara Jane winced as he penetrated her. She let out one yelp of pain, then a big smile wreathed her face. She nodded and began to pant, and her hips danced below him, pumping up at him and urging him to drive into her.

"I'm not hurting you?"

"Fuck, no, just keep humping. Makes a difference when I want it. I'm so hot I think I might burn your big cock right off you. Do me, Buckskin, fuck me harder!"

Buckskin did. Sara Jane suddenly whooped and screamed, then tore into a climax that shook her and glazed her eyes and brought huge gasps from her as she tried to get her breath. Her whole body trembled and vibrated like she was tearing herself apart.

Then she quieted down, gave a big sigh and looked up at Buckskin with a grin. "Now that was a do. I loved that. Nobody ever made me tear into tiny pieces that way before."

Just then Buckskin gloriously erupted and pounded against her six times before he fell on top of her, so exhausted that he couldn't move.

After a few minutes, she unwound her arms from his back and he rolled away from her.

"Now that was really something. Not even my James ever done me so good. I can't figure it out, but I enjoyed the hell out of it. Soon as you're ready I want to try to make that kind of magic come again."

Buckskin at last had his breath back, and he sat there on the floor watching her. She sat up as well, not the least bit embarrassed by her nakedness. She caught one of his hands and brought it to her breasts.

"So, what do you think? Is the poon good enough to convince you to teach me how to kill those three bastards who murdered my James and raped me?"

"It was great, but that has nothing to do with whether or not I teach you how to shoot a six-gun so you can go out and get yourself killed. What makes you think you can track down these three desperados and do away with them? How many men have you killed?"

"Ain't killed nobody, but don't look too hard. Cock the hammer and pull the trigger. That forty-five slug does the killing. Ain't saying I could do it with a knife."

"But you've never killed anything bigger than a chicken, have you?"

"No, but I'm willing to learn. First, I want you to teach me how to shoot better. I don't want no big forty-five. Something smaller, not so heavy."

Buckskin shook his head. "Just ain't right, you trying to do a man's work. Chances are three to one that one of them you try to kill will kill you. Not good odds in my gambling book."

"They won't know who I am or what I'm about to do. I'll surprise them. I'll change my hair and wear fancy clothes, and they won't even suspect until I belly shoot them. Then when they're groveling in the dirt asking for mercy, I'll make sure they know it's me and I'll blow their brains all over the countryside, the way they did to my James."

"You won't have it any other way?"

She turned shyly, covering up her breasts with her arms. "Sir, you've had your way with me. You might have made me pregnant. You owe me a certain amount of time and effort for my giving myself to you."

Buckskin laughed. "That one won't work. You practically raped me. You were the one who wanted to have sex all the time."

She laughed and stood so her breasts shook and her swatch of brown hair barely covered the flash of pink at her crotch.

"I sure did, and you loved it. I'm going to put on some more practical clothes. I've got pants I cut down and some shirts. Today you're going to teach me how to shoot. I've got a thirty-eight caliber hidden away and two boxes of cartridges."

She turned so he could see the profile of her breasts and paused. "Like what you see, cowboy? It's all yours for the next week or so while you train me to be a woman who can fight as good as any man. You rest up from your terrible ordeal here on the floor and I'll be back in a few minutes ready to start my training."

Buckskin held up his hand, stopping her.

"But can you cook? I demand three squares a day when I'm training a raw beginner to be an awesome, unstoppable killer."

Sara Jane grinned. "Yes, Mr. Morgan, I can cook. I can cook and I can fuck good, and that should be enough to hold you for a week or more." She chuckled and hurried her bare bottom to the other side of the room where she dug into a chest of drawers.

Twenty minutes later, Buckskin checked out the .38 Remington six-gun she handed him. It was almost new, and he doubted that more than a dozen rounds had been fired through it. He tested the action, broke it open and showed her how to put one .38 cartridge in a cylinder, then gave it to her to finish loading it.

"Just five rounds," he cautioned. "That's so the hammer can rest on an empty chamber when not in use. If the hammer was on a live round and you dropped the piece, the hammer could jolt backward and then return to the round and fire it. Safety move."

She finished the fifth round and pushed the cylinder back in place. He opened it and told her to move the empty chamber to the top of the weapon so it would be in place for the hammer to rest on.

"Start with the well house over there," Buckskin said. "It's six feet square. Can you hit it from here?"

They stood 20 feet away. Sara Jane lifted the weapon and, holding it with both hands, aimed down the sights and pulled the trigger. The pull of her finger swept the weapon to the right, and the round missed the building.

Patiently he showed her how not to jerk the trigger but to squeeze it gently until it tripped the hammer. She fired ten rounds, the last eight hitting the small building.

He looked at her. "No holster for the weapon? How will you carry it—in your reticule?"

"I could. There's a holster and gunbelt inside made for this weapon. Now let's get on with the lesson."

Buckskin set up two cardboard boxes he found in the woodshed beside the house. He put them on the ground 20 feet away. One was a foot square, the other one two feet square.

"Now, aim at those smaller targets. We'll work down to tin cans soon enough. Can you hold the weapon with one hand?"

She tried and missed the biggest box. Then she used both hands and hit the big box, tumbling it backwards. She grinned, tried the smaller box and knocked that over as well.

Buckskin went into the house and brought out a three-foot-high stool. He put the smaller box on top of that and stood beside it.

"Always aim at the largest part of the target. On a man, that's his chest. That's also where his heart and lungs are, and a slug through either one, or his belly, will put him down and screaming. Try the small box."

She adjusted her aim to the higher target and knocked it off the stool four out of five times, using her two-handed grip.

Buckskin nodded. "All right, keep that two-handed way of shooting. It's slower, but you won't be in much of a rush most of the time. Make certain you hit your target whether it's a box on a stool or a killer."

"Dinnertime," Sara Jane said. She turned, hurried to the kitchen and looked in a small cupboard. "Ham and cheese sandwich and dill pickles and coffee for dinner. For supper I'll wring a chicken's neck, and we'll have all the fried chicken you can eat. We eat a lot of chicken because none of the meat spoils." She paused and brushed tears from her cheeks.

"We used to eat chickens, James and me. The two of us could polish off most of a chicken in the evening and save the bones and rest of it for a chicken stew. Made two meals out of one chicken."

After supper, she washed the dishes in water heated on the stove, then sat down near the lamp she had lit on the kitchen table and poured Buckskin a second cup of coffee.

"You never did say if you'd stay or not and teach me what I need to know."

"You never gave me a chance."

She laughed softly and touched his shoulder. "I know. I get pushy that way sometimes. You've saved me once already. I had decided to shoot myself after they left and I saw the barn burning and knew James was dead. That's why I had out the six-gun."

"You've got a lot to live for, young lady."

Sara Jane smiled and reached for his crotch. "I know, and I like this part of it especially."

Buckskin caught her hand. "You're behaving like a bride on her wedding night."

She lifted her brows and then nodded. "Yep, you're right. I just never knew it could be so good. With James it was always after dark, in bed where we couldn't even see each other."

Sara Jane sipped her coffee. "So can you stay a week or so?"

"As long as the cooking holds up. I'm tired of eating my own trail food."

"Hey, we'll do fine. You didn't look in my pantry. Maybe we can do the training in three days; then I won't be so far behind them killers."

Buckskin stood and leaned against the back of his chair, facing her. "Damn, I knew I never should have stopped here. I should have just ridden past and forgotten about it."

"But you didn't, because you're good and fine and honest and upstanding and . . ." She stopped. "And you're just wonderful when it comes to poking me. I can't wait until it's bedtime." She grinned at him. "No chance I'm letting you sleep on the floor tonight."

The next day Buckskin was to teach the lady how to ride. He swept around the home range for three miles and at last found two more cow ponies he herded back to the corral. He picked the smaller of the two, saddled the mare and rode her. She was gentle, well-broken and not the skittish type.

Buckskin concentrated on the basics of riding long distances, and Sara Jane caught on quickly. She kept her weight forward, sat tall in the saddle and developed a light touch on the reins.

The next day they did some tracking, but Buckskin figured the three killers would spend most of their time in some town somewhere between here and Phoenix or in Phoenix itself, so he gave her only some of the basics about tracking a horse.

That night in bed she rolled over on top of him and kissed his lips gently. "Tomorrow we start out to find those three gents who killed James."

Buckskin scowled. "I reckon I can't stop you, but I can slow you down if you head into something I don't think you can handle. Promise me that you won't call it square if you kill all three but die yourself in the process."

Sara Jane thought about that a minute. Slowly she shook her head. "A few days ago I would have settled for that, but now I see that if I do that, they win again. I'm tired of losing all the time. I want to win this little battle. No, I won't get killed myself just to take them to boot hill in a handcart."

They had a quick breakfast the next morning; then Sara Jane pried up a floorboard and took out a glass jar. She counted the money inside it—a little over $50.

"Not even James knew about this," she told Buckskin. "I had it from savings a long time ago as an emergency fund. Now we can put it to good use."

She had shown him her husband's Greener double-barreled shotgun. He found a hacksaw in the shed that didn't burn down and sawed off both barrels so the whole weapon was only two feet long. They took the Greener and two boxes of double-aught buck. Buckskin had his Spencer 7-shot carbine in the .52 caliber and brought a Winchester .45 from the house. He felt better armed than in a long time.

They rode out just after dawn. She had baked loaves of bread for them to take along and also some cans of beans and a jar of jam she had made months before from crab apples.

Twice they had practiced tracking, heading out on the three sets of prints the killers had left when they rode away from the Nelson ranch.

This morning they kept going along the set of prints. There had been no rain recently and the winds had settled down a little, so the trail was easy to follow down the grade and toward the valley in the distant haze.

"What's the next little town in this direction?" Buckskin asked.

"San Carlos Wells. Maybe three hundred people live there. I could never figure out why. It's where we went to do our shopping and get supplies when we could afford them. It's about fifteen miles from the ranch."

"Tell me about this Something Smith and the other two. I'd like to be able to spot them if I see them."

"I'll never forget any of them. Smith is a big one, an inch or so over six feet. He's lean and mean with a big head of white hair. Stands out like a beacon. He was clean-shaven and had little beady red eyes. Smith just looks bad as soon as you see him."

"Let's hope we don't see him until we're ready to."

Sara Jane carried a small carpetbag tied on the back of her saddle and now rode in jeans and a shirt. The .38 six-gun rode in leather on her right thigh.

Buckskin hoped they were ready.

They made it to town slightly before noon. Buckskin had no idea why so many people had gathered in that barren, dry little valley either. They were still 60 miles from Phoenix in the edge of the Mescal mountains that brooded away mostly to the north. Buckskin saw a sign that pointed south and east to Tucson.

They had talked about camping outside of town, but there was no stream of any kind. They settled for the second best looking hotel in the village and took one room. Buckskin signed in as Mr. and Mrs. L. Morgan.

They had just started up to their room when Sara Jane whispered something. He didn't hear and looked at her.

"I think I just saw one of them. Larson, they called him. He's the one with a black patch over his left eye, and he just went into the hotel dining room."

Chapter Three

Buckskin Morgan looked at Sara Jane Nelson quickly. "Are you sure you saw one of the killers?"

"Absolutely. He had a patch over his left eye. I'll never forget that face staring down at me when I lay tied down on my bed." She broke off and turned away.

"Let's go see about it," Buckskin said. They went to the door of the dining room and looked in. It wasn't a large area, seating no more than 30. The man with the patch over his left eye sat at a table facing them as he read a menu.

"That's him," Sara Jane whispered. She edged behind Buckskin so the man couldn't see her. After a long look to make sure he could identify the man again, Buckskin turned and pulled Sara Jane away.

"I want to go in there and shoot him dead," Sara Jane said. "I can do it before he knows I'm there."

"No good," Buckskin said. "You do that and you'll hang for murder. What happened back at the ranch won't matter here. You'd get at least thirty years in the territorial prison. You can't do it here."

She tugged to get away, but he held her fast. They were still in their riding clothes and her .38 revolver lay in leather on her right thigh.

"Don't reach for that iron or we're both in trouble. We go up to our room and get settled. Then we'll come down and follow him when he leaves the dining room. Then you should have a chance at him."

Sara Jane pouted as they went to room 212 on the second floor.

Inside, she sat on the bed and stared at the wall, her hands clenching and opening and clenching again. "All I could think of was him on top of me, and I wanted to rush right in there and blast away at him." She took a long, deep breath. "I can still smell his foul breath, see his blackened, rotting teeth, feel him . . ." She looked away and took another deep breath.

"Oh, damn."

Buckskin put their carpetbags on the bed beside her and sat in the one wooden chair. "He'll be there at least a half hour. In ten minutes we'll go down and wait for him. You'll be in the lobby and I'll be in the restaurant, having a cup of coffee and watching him. When he leaves, I'll come out behind him and you'll follow me."

Slowly Sara Jane nodded. Her green eyes shot off sparks, and she trembled, evidently still trying to control the fury that flashed through her. She glanced at Buckskin.

"I understand. I don't want to get jailed at least until I kill all three. With Larson, I'll wait my chance."

Sara Jane changed from her jeans to a brown town dress, not the least bit embarrassed undressing in front of him. For just a moment she looked at him when she wore only her chemise and short bloomers, then she lifted her brows as much as if to say they could make love later. She combed out her long hair and took from her carpetbag a medium-sized reticule that was big enough to hold her .38. Then she glanced at Buckskin.

"I'm ready. Shouldn't we be going?"

A few minutes later, Buckskin found a place for her to sit in the small lobby where she could see the dining room door, and he went into the eatery. He had just passed the door and scanned the room, when he realized that the man with the black eye patch was not there. He stopped at the small desk where a cashier sat and nodded.

"Evening. I was supposed to meet a man here. He had a black eye patch on. Has he come yet?"

The woman behind the counter smiled. "Indeed he did. Came and ordered a dinner on a tin plate and took it out to eat somewhere else. Man seemed a bit on edge."

Buckskin thanked her, hurried back to Sara Jane and sat down beside her.

"You lost him," she said.

He explained what happened. "We'll just have to keep our eyes out for him. At least we know one of them is still here in San Carlos Wells. We'll find him. This isn't that big a place. Let me see if he's registered here in the hotel."

The hotel clerk was helpful, but he said he was sure that the man wasn't registered. The only time he'd seen him was when he came in for some food and then left by the side door not ten minutes ago.

Sara Jane scowled, then pounded her fist into the couch and looked at Buckskin. "Something I haven't told you. I heard one of them say something about a judge. It sounded like Something Smith was mad at one of the others and he said, 'We'll do this job just the way the judge told us to.' Any idea what that could mean?"

Buckskin shook his head. "Small town like this wouldn't have a judge, excepting maybe a circuit judge of some kind who came twice a year. There'd be a judge in Phoenix, but that's another sixty miles or so."

Sara Jane stood and began pacing the area in front of the couch. "So where do we start to look for Larson? If he bought a meal here he took it somewhere close by to eat it."

"That could be lots of places. Let me go talk with the town marshal or sheriff or whatever they have here. You can look at the pretty things in one of the stores."

It turned out to be a town marshal. The county sheriff was in Phoenix. As with most territories, the founding fathers had carved Arizona into only a few large counties, so it wouldn't take so much organization and so many elections to get ready to become a territory. Since that time not much had been done to split the big counties into smaller ones.

Buckskin explained his search.

"Yep, I've heard of the three. Call themselves the Something Smith gang. Smith collects lowlife to help him do his dirty work.

"I've got paper on them for robbery and murder, but don't recollect seeing them in town. Oh, they been in and out, but they move fast, never stay out this way for long. Hear tell that they spend most of their time in Phoenix."

"Know what they look like?" Buckskin asked.

"Something Smith is a big guy, six one or so, lean and mean. Got a shock of white hair. Says he got it when he was struck by lightning one day. No beard. I've heard he's got a big nose and small, beady eyes."

"Tallies with what I hear. Oh, don't know if you keep records or not, but Smith and his gang killed James Nelson at the Nelson ranch about fifteen miles east of here few days back."

"Yep, sounds like Smith. Probably did it for whatever cash they could steal. Another one in the bunch is Willy Pointer. He's a damn crazy who should be hung twice. He's shit-ass mean and nasty. Don't ever turn your back on that one."

The lawman wrote something on a pad of paper. "I'll make a note of the killing and report it to the sheriff in Phoenix. He won't do nothing about it, but I'll send along the message anyway. You see the killing?"

"No, but Sara Jane Nelson, the widow, did. She was in the same room."

"Put that down, too. Sheriff over in Phoenix ain't exactly the best lawman in the world, but he gets elected. You gonna be in town long?"

"Couple of days. The widow is resting up after burying her husband."

"Watch out for them three. They strike without warning, play dirty, kill any way they can without giving their victims a chance. All three are wanted for murder in the territory. Slippery as soap on a hot stone." The marshal nodded at Buckskin. "You be careful now, y'hear?"

Buckskin left the office and went back to the store where he had left Sara Jane. She had bought a new dress and a fancy hat and had a radiant smile he hadn't seen on her before.

"When we find them varmints, I want to be all gussied up so they don't know me at first. Make it easier to get in range of my .38 and blow them to hell."

Buckskin told her what he'd found out from the marshal.

"So, I think it's time you buy a ticket to Denver where you said you had a brother. You can have him come back and help you with the ranch. Forget this idea of finding them three rattlesnakes."

"Buckskin Morgan, you don't know me. I've got a lot of Irish in me, and we don't knuckle under to a trio of rattlesnakes. Right now I'd rather curl up and die rather than let them get away with murdering my husband. I'm here until I get them or they get me. Now, do you still want to help me or not? Either way I'm on their trail, and I've got two boxes of .38 rounds."

Buckskin groaned. He held the door open for her, and they stepped out to the boardwalk. He stopped, faced her, put both fists on his hips and frowned.

"Damn it all, Sara Jane, you're as pigheaded as a mule I used to fight with. A lot prettier, though. Nothing else I can do now but hang around and make sure you're not shot full of holes. I'd truly hate to have to go to your funeral." He gave a big sigh and looked at the heavens.

"Reckon the first thing we should do is try to find your friend, old one-eye."

"How?"

"First, we'll check the other hotel. Larson is an easy man to remember with that eye patch. The room clerk might come up with something if I can find a spare silver dollar."

The room clerk remembered, but he hadn't seen Larson anywhere in his establishment. That left the boarding houses. They stopped at the general store where Buckskin bought a box of .45 rounds. When he paid for them he inquired about boarding houses in town. The woman behind the counter nodded.

"Smart way to go before you buy a place of your own. Get to know the town and see if you like it. There are four of them that take in folks. I'll write them down for you with their addresses. We like to help each other out in San Carlos Wells, and these ladies are all widows and can use the business."

They walked through the whole town which was only three blocks long and two wide. Two of the ladies were home but had not rented a room to a man with an eye patch. The other two places were at the other end of town.

"Let me check in on a couple of saloons as we go past," Buckskin said. "Larson seems the kind of gent who would be a steady patron of the bar."

The first barkeep shook his head when asked about Larson. Said nobody with an eye patch had been in his place in a couple of years.

The next apron snorted when Buckskin asked him.

"Hell, yes, he's around. Was in here last night. Put three new bullet holes in my ceiling and I had to have him thrown out. Said it was time he hit the best bordello in town anyway.

"Which one is that?"

"Hilda's Emporium of Pussy Delights. That sign is inside. Outside it just says Hilda's. A block over, a few steps off Main."

Buckskin thanked him and found Sara Jane staring in a window of a women's wear store.

They checked the next boarding house where the owner said yes, she did have a man with a patch over his eye, a Mr. Sanderson. He said he'd be staying for a week.

"Don't tell him we asked about him. We're friends of his from Phoenix and want to surprise him for his birthday. You know how family is. We'll come back tonight when he'll be here. Does he usually come to supper?"

"Oh, yes, he never misses."

They thanked the lady and walked back to the middle of town.

"So, we know where he'll be for supper," Buckskin said. "After supper he'll be full and a little slow and probably head downtown for some amusement. Be few people on the street around here. Does that sound like a good time to confront him?"

Her eyes glinted. "A perfect time." She looked around at the street. "Right back there, half a block from the boarding house. See how that shed sticks out toward the street? I could be there waiting for him. He'd pass within ten feet of me. He couldn't see me until he was abreast of me. A perfect spot."

She nodded, smiling grimly. "I think we might pick off the first of the killers with little or no trouble and no danger of being seen."

"You might want to ask him where the other two went before you kill him." Buckskin smiled at her.

"What? No, I know what you're thinking—that I won't be able to do the job once I get that close to him. All I need to do is remember what he did to James and to me, and I'll pull the trigger twice."

"That's a single action piece. Remember to cock the hammer between shots or you'll just fire it once."

They continued down the street.

Sara Jane pulled at Buckskin's shirt sleeve. "You really don't think I'll be able to shoot him, do you?"

Buckskin stopped and locked his gaze on hers. "Killing a man isn't as simple as it sounds. You're taking a human life. No matter how lowdown and rotten that person may be, he's still a human being. Some folks don't think there are enough of us to go around as it is. Others maintain that the bad ones should be shot dead or hanged for their crimes. Just got to pick which way you think and walk down that path."

"But you've killed men."

"How do you know?"

"By the way you talk. You go all around the subject and use a lot of fancy words. All I know is they killed James and done me twice each, and I'm gonna kill them. Now, do you want to find something to eat or are we going to starve ourselves all day?"

"We didn't have dinner, did we?" Buckskin asked.

They found a small café and had some vegetable soup which was surprisingly good.

Buckskin took a second biscuit and soaked up the rest of his soup.

When their coffee was finished, Buckskin checked his Waterbury. It was 15 minutes to five o'clock.

"Best we get back to that boarding house. I'll hold back a bit in case you get yourself in trouble. I still don't like the idea of you taking on a killer with that little pop gun of yours."

"My .38 will do nicely. I figure one round right through his heart, then I'll fade back down that little alley place, cut between houses and be back on Main Street before anybody knows that Larson is a dead man."

"Let's hope, Sara Jane, let's hope."

Buckskin was pleased the way Sara Jane got to her selected spot and moved back into some small shrubs to be out of sight of anyone coming either direction on the sidewalk. He found a place 30 feet farther away from her ambush spot and eased down behind a low stone wall.

They waited.

Buckskin checked his pocket watch. It was 6:30 and Larson had not come home to supper. He missed his evening meal that was all paid for at a dollar a day. Now what? Larson might not come back until late tonight.

Buckskin slid out from his hiding spot and ambled down the dirt track of a street, then turned and walked to where Sara Jane waited.

"Why are you here?" she demanded in a whisper.

"Larson has missed supper. A boarding house doesn't feed latecomers. Larson won't be back this way until he's ready to get some sleep, or maybe not at all. I hear he spends some money over at Hilda's Emporium, a bawdy house."

"Well, I'm not going in there to look for him, but I bet you wouldn't mind checking out the hookers to find out if Larson is there tonight."

"Might. A little early for Larson, I'd guess. Why don't I take a look at the saloons first. He might play poker, never can tell."

"What am I supposed to do, wait outside?"

"You can wait here and hope he comes home early, or go back to that café and have a long

three cups of coffee. I'll meet you there if I find
him."

"I could go back to the hotel."

"Could, but won't. Larson has to go home sometime. Now's as good a chance as we'll have. Wait in
the café where we ate. I'll be there when I know
something."

Sara Jane frowned, her bottom lip sticking out
in a pout like she was five again. It was starting
to get dark. At last she shrugged, stood up from
where she had been sitting and moved ahead of
him on the way back to Main Street.

They then parted, Buckskin heading for the
closest saloon and Sara Jane for the Desert
Inn Café.

Buckskin ordered a beer at the bar and let his
eyes adjust to the dim light. The only lamps were
those on the poker tables and two on the bar.

He sipped at his beer and surveyed the place.
Two poker games were going, four men in each.
He eased closer. He was about to ask for a seat
at one table when a man came through the rear
door and slid into a chair where a stack of chips
had been left.

"I'm back. Deal the damn cards," the man
said.

Buckskin looked at the player closer in the dim
light. He had a black patch over his left eye. This
was the same man Sara Jane had pointed out as
Larson.

Buckskin pulled out a chair across from Larson.
"Is this a closed game or can a man with twenty
dollars sit in?"

"New money," Larson said. "More than damn
welcome."

The others nodded or waved, and Buckskin sat
down, dropping the gold double eagle on the table.

"Anybody want to sell me some chips?" Buckskin had learned more about men by the way they played poker than any other way. He took the chips and settled into the game, watching the killer who sat across from him.

Chapter Four

The poker game was not the best quality. There was a quarter limit on bets. The first hand resulted in a pot of a little over two dollars, and Larson won it. Buckskin watched when Larson dealt the next hand, but he didn't show any of the usual methods of cheating.

Buckskin won the next hand of about four dollars and then settled back, watching the men around the table. It was mediocre poker. Buckskin decided if he wanted to bluff enough he could win four out of five hands.

Larson was the man who bet the most, raised the most and had the most chips on the table.

An hour later, Larson checked a pocket watch, folded his hand and cashed in his chips with the barkeep. He looked like a winner.

Buckskin waited until Larson was outside, then bowed out of the game and cashed in. He had won $15.

He hurried out the door and spotted Sara Jane pacing in front of the hardware store next to the saloon. It was fully dark now, and Buckskin walked toward her and called her name so he wouldn't startle her. Then they walked down the street.

"You were supposed to wait in the café."

"It closed and you weren't there. Besides I saw Larson come out a few minutes ago and head straight for that whorehouse you talked about—Hilda's."

"He's there now?"

"He is, and who knows if he'll ever come out?"

"I'll go in and see. Chances are he's upstairs already."

Sara Jane frowned. "You don't feel funny . . . going in a place like that?"

"Not at all. I'm not going to be a paying customer. Don't think a man should have to pay for his loving."

He looked at Sara Jane and figured she was blushing in the darkness.

"I'll talk to the madam and find out if my cousin is in there and when he'll be coming out."

"You can do that?"

He held out a five dollar bill and let her see it in the light splattering out the saloon window. "Amazing what a five dollar bill will buy these days. Lots of information." He looked around. Nothing was left open except the saloons. He walked with her to the whorehouse and marched her into the darkness near the side of the building.

"You stay right here and don't move. Nobody will see you, so you'll be as safe as if you were in your granny's kitchen. I'll be back in ten minutes."

He walked up to Hilda's door and pulled it open. Buckskin found himself in a small entryway that led into what at one time had been the family parlor. It was not fancied up but simply had wallpaper on ceiling and walls, three couches and a few chairs. In the far corner was a softly tinkling piano played by a man with garters holding up his long shirtsleeves, a big cigar hanging out of his mouth and a black derby covering up his lack of hair. Buckskin guessed the man was in his sixties.

Three girls sat on the sofas, each wearing a robe of sorts but draped so each one exposed one bare breast. Buckskin had taken only two steps into the room when a small woman with a figure like a broomstick marched in from a door leading off to the right.

"Yes, sir, how may we serve you? If you're looking for some fine entertainment, you've come to the right place. Hilda's is the place where no man goes unpleased."

Her hair was dark with traces of gray and cropped close to her head to give her a manly look. She wore a dress that fell straight from her shoulders to her ankles with no breasts or hips to get in the way. If she had any breasts or hips they were well-hidden.

"Your office?" Buckskin asked.

The woman's sharp features grew even sharper, but she motioned him back the way she had come.

Her office was a small room that had walls that went to the ceiling, but they were patchwork and looked temporary.

The room held a small desk and two chairs. She sat behind the desk and stared at him.

"You a lawman or something?"

"Something," Buckskin said and grinned. "A guy I know came in a few minutes ago. You probably know him. Wears a black patch over his left eye."

"Yeah, I know the sonofabitch. You gonna pay for the damage to my house and my girl?"

"Not so you would notice. Just wondered how long he usually stays and when I can expect him outside."

Her face edged into a frown, then she shrugged. "Hell, I hope you put a slug in the creep. He pays, but I wish he would go away. Usual he's with Patsy for about an hour. She says he's as slow as a jackass pissing backwards. So, about an hour. That fiver for me?"

"It is." Buckskin hadn't bothered to sit down. He dropped the bill on her desk and turned.

"Oh, might warn you. The man's a killer. He's a no good bastard so you best be careful. Calls himself a rattlesnake and says he strikes without warning. You be more than careful. Hate to see a fine looking man like you out in our boot hill."

"Obliged," Buckskin said and walked out of her office, waving at the two girls still in the parlor. One of them opened her robe from top to bottom in a sales effort. Her breasts were good, but she had a fat little tummy that spoiled the effect.

"Not today, ladies," he said and walked out the front door. He picked up Sara Jane at the corner of the building, and they walked back toward town.

"He's usually there about an hour," Buckskin said. "That gives you some time to set up your ambush. Where will you be, and what will you do?"

"But . . ." She frowned in the darkness, and he saw traces of her scowl in the soft moonlight. She

looked up and down the street. They were nearly
half a block off Main. Only two buildings were
on each side of the street between the whorehouse and Main. That left empty gaps between
them.

Sara Jane pointed to the other side of the street.
"He'll come out and head for the saloons. All three
are to the left of here, so he crosses the street to get
there quicker. I'll be waiting behind the blind side
of that first building. I'll wait until he gets near
the building, then walk toward him until he sees
that I'm a woman. I'll be holding the gun at my
side. When I get within ten feet of him, I'll lift the
weapon, hold it with both hands and shoot him
dead."

"Good luck," Buckskin said.

They came to the building she had picked. She
stepped along the far side and then peered around
the corner. Sara Jane nodded. "Yes, this should
work. I'd bet anything that he'll come across the
street at an angle and be near this building when
he heads for Main."

"Fine."

"You don't believe me."

"You wanted to do it yourself."

She stamped her small foot on the ground,
but it made no sound. "You can be so mean
sometimes."

"Wait until you've killed three men."

She looked at him, then turned away. Sara
Jane stepped to the corner of the building and
peered around it, watching the whorehouse. A
man came out.

She frowned.

Soundlessly, Buckskin moved in behind her.
He touched her shoulder and looked around the
corner with her.

"Another small problem. In the dark, how are you going to be sure that the man who comes this way is Larson?"

"Oh, that *will* be hard." She turned back. "But if I can't do it in broad daylight, and I can't identify him for certain in the dark, how can I kill him?"

"You're starting to get the idea."

She turned to him, tears brimming in her eyes. "What can I do?"

"You can let me help you just a little. All right?"

She nodded.

"We wait until the hour is almost up, then we begin to stop everyone who comes this way on some pretext or another until we find Larson. Shouldn't be too hard to spot with the eye patch. I'll cover him while you get his six-gun out of leather. Then we'll march him out in the desert a ways and have a long chat with him about who the judge is."

Sara Jane stared at him in the moonlight and slowly bobbed her head. "Yes, let's do it that way."

"No tricks. We capture him, disarm him and take him out of town a ways."

"Fine, no tricks."

They waited. Buckskin lit a match and checked his Waterbury. It had been 50 minutes since he had left Hilda's. A man came out the door, stretched and then walked straight toward them. Buckskin went out of the shadows into the street. Sara Jane stayed where she was.

Buckskin quickly saw this was the wrong man, so he angled away from him, circled around and went back to the vacant store.

"Not him," Buckskin whispered.

Another man left the whorehouse. This time the man was Larson, eye patch and all. Morgan walked almost to him, then brought his Colt from behind his back and pushed it into Larson's gut.

"Don't move or make a sound, Larson, or you're a dead man."

"Who the hell?"

"No questions. I'll take your hardware." Buckskin drew out Larson's six-gun and pushed it in his own belt, then turned Larson around.

"Going for a little stroll out of town," Buckskin said. He saw Sara Jane coming up from behind them. They walked slowly and passed a few houses. Then the wilderness took over with cactus and sagebrush and rocky soil.

Sara Jane caught up with them and made sure it was Larson, not just a man with an eye patch.

She looked at him closely in the soft moonlight, then bellowed in anger.

"You bastard, Larson! You murdered my husband in cold blood. You shot down James Nelson like he was a gopher that got in your way."

Larson grunted. "Crazy bitch. Keep her away from me. I don't know who you are, mister, but keep this crazy woman away from me."

Buckskin turned to watch Sara Jane to be sure she didn't do something wild. At the same instant, Larson brayed in fear and anger and broke away from Buckskin.

Sara Jane must already have had her .38 up ready to fire. She pulled the trigger twice with Larson no more than 20 feet ahead of her. One of the rounds hit him in the shoulder, and he stumbled and went down, roaring with pain.

"That bitch shot me! That crazy woman shot me."

When Buckskin caught Sara Jane's .38 in one hand, she let go of it. He grabbed Larson by his good arm and pushed him forward.

"We still need a little chat with you, killer. Don't try to get away again, or I'll be the one drawing down on you—and I won't just hit your arm. Now move."

Five minutes later they came to a decline where Buckskin pushed Larson to the ground and glared at him in the moonlight.

"Now, Larson, time to talk. You're one of the three men who murdered James Nelson four days ago. One of the others was Something Smith. We want to know who the third one was."

Larson snorted. "Why the hell should I tell you?"

Sara Jane doubled up her fist and swung it as hard as she could, pounding it into Larson's wounded shoulder. He bellowed in pain, and tears came out of his eyes.

"That's one good reason to tell us, Larson," Sara Jane said. "I saw you torture my James. I'm ready to do the same thing to you for as long as it takes."

"No, no more. He's Willy Pointer. Everyone knows he rides with Something Smith."

Buckskin Morgan nodded. "Fine, now we want to know who the judge is and where he is."

"What judge?"

Sara Jane hit his shoulder again, and he fell to the ground bleating in pain. Slowly he sat up.

"Don't know who this judge is. Smith might. He was the guy who got paid. Don't hit me again."

Sara Jane had her six-gun back again. She eased it in and out of the holster.

"Next time I hit you with the butt of my six-gun, Larson," Sara Jane said. "You don't know what hurt feels like. After that I shoot you in the knee the way you did James."

"No, no," Larson said. "Don't hit my shoulder. I'll tell you about the judge, then you'll take me to a doctor, right? Damn, that hurts." He bent forward again, and Buckskin saw him fumbling at his leg just over his boot.

A hideout! Buckskin thought. He dug for his Colt knowing he wouldn't be in time. As Larson came up with a derringer and lifted it toward Sara Jane, a gun went off.

Larson gasped, dropped the hideout and put both hands over his chest. Then he fell over backwards into the Arizona sand and dirt.

Buckskin looked at Sara Jane. She held the .38 in both hands, still covering Larson. Buckskin knelt down beside the man and touched his throat for a pulse, then pinched his nose.

"Put away your piece. Larson is dead."

Sara Jane calmly holstered her weapon, stood there a moment looking down at Larson, then rushed into Buckskin's arms, tears streaming down her face.

"I killed him! Oh, God, I killed him dead. He came at me with that little gun, but I know how deadly they are. I had to shoot him or he would have shot me and then you. I had to shoot him. I already had my gun out, just wishing I had the nerve to kill him. Oh, God, I just killed a man."

She then cried so hard that she couldn't speak. She wailed and half-screamed out her shock and her anger at herself and at Larson.

Buckskin stood there holding her. Her tears wet his shoulder, and she burrowed deeper against him as if trying to hide from what she had done.

Slowly her anger subsided, and her crying tapered off. She still held Buckskin tightly. Finally she eased back from him and wiped the wetness from her face.

"Oh, God, I killed him! I didn't know what it would feel like. He's gone. Larson has ceased to exist. You were right. Killing someone changes a person. Oh, damn! I tried to kill him before, when he ran, but I missed. This time . . ."

Buckskin led her away. They had stayed near the body too long as it was. Nobody might be interested in a couple of shots in the night, but then again someone might. He walked in a half-circle around the few lights he could see of the town, then came in between two houses to a dirt street and found Main.

A few minutes later they closed the door to their hotel room and tried to relax. They sat side by side on the bed without saying a word. She reached over and held his hand. A minute later she leaned her head on his shoulder.

"I feel so strange. I'm tired, but I'm so high-strung I could never go to sleep. I know that I just killed a man, and that makes me sad, but I'm elated that one of James' killers is roasting right now in hell. I feel chilled, but at the same time a fire burns inside me that I know will never go out until all three of those killers are dead.

"I feel so alone, yet at the same time I have a driving urge to make love to you. Am I crazy, Lee Buckskin Morgan? Am I losing my mind?"

He put his arm around her, and she snuggled against him, turning her face up to him. He kissed her gently on her lips.

"You're not crazy, Sara Jane Nelson. You're reacting to a violent, terrible experience. What you're going through is natural and normal. I'd be surprised if it didn't affect you at all. The bad parts will fade and go away."

She kissed him again, then they lay back on the bed. She pushed against him and murmured softly in her throat.

"Please, Buckskin, make love to me ever so gently and softly and lovingly. Make me feel like a bride, like it was my first time ever. Love me and help make me well."

Chapter Five

They undressed and slipped beneath the sheet but for the moment didn't touch. Then Sara Jane rolled toward him, held his face and kissed him softly. She sighed and curled against his chest, her arms around him, holding him tight.

They stayed that way for 15 minutes until Morgan stirred. She turned and kissed his bare chest, then cuddled against him.

"I feel so secure, so protected, so safe this way, Buckskin. Is it all right if we just stay this way for a while?"

"Yes, of course." He bent down and kissed her soft brown hair. He felt her relax, and a moment later she slept. He tried to move her away from him but she whimpered, so he remained with her clinging tightly to him.

About midnight she let go of him and turned over, sleeping on her side. A moment later she cried out, sat bolt upright in bed and came awake.

She turned at once, saw him in the dim light of the room and let out a small cry of delight. Quickly she pushed against him, rested her head on his chest and took a deep breath. A second later Sara Jane fell asleep again.

At six-thirty A.M., Buckskin came awake slowly. He found his arm aching from its cramped position, cradling Sara Jane. He couldn't remember getting much sleep. Twice during the night she had let out a scream and sat up in bed. When she saw him there she pressed against him again and promptly went to sleep.

It was the strangest night Buckskin had ever spent in bed with a woman. It was her reaction to killing Larson. He wondered if the one kill would satisfy her, or if she would insist on trying for the other two, the more dangerous of the trio.

She awoke a minute later, rolled over and stared at him. She frowned. "Sorry I wasn't better company last night. As I remember, about the sexiest thing that happened was when I kissed you. Was that it?"

"You don't remember?"

"Don't tease me, Morgan, not yet. I admit that I'm still a little bit shaky. It's not every day that I kill another human being and send him straight to hell."

She sat up. "I actually did shoot him—kill him—didn't I?" She looked at him for confirmation.

"You did. I suggest we catch the ten o'clock stage for Phoenix. Unless you want to ride on that horse another sixty miles."

"Oh, no, the stage, please."

"We'll have breakfast, then I'll sell our horses to the livery and bring my saddle and get tickets on the stage."

Sara Jane nodded her approval.

The 60 miles to Phoenix took just a little over eight hours. By changing horses every ten miles at swing stations, the stage could average almost eight miles an hour. They had one half-hour food stop at a little town nearly halfway, then loaded back on the big Conestoga stage for the rest of the ride. Only six people rode inside, which meant all had seats with backs on them and no one had to sit on the backless bench in the center of the coach.

The ride was rough and bruising, but it was faster and better than riding a horse that far, Sara Jane told him.

In Phoenix they found a modest hotel, took a room on the second floor and washed up. Then they had a late supper in the dining room just before it closed.

It was after nine o'clock before they got back to their room. Sara Jane was exhausted and sat on the edge of the bed, bleary-eyed and limp.

"Do I have to get undressed to go to bed?" she asked.

"Not at all. I'll be glad to do the job for you."

She flashed him a smile. "No, then we'd be three hours making love before we could get to sleep. I'm feeling much more alive and sensitive to that sort of thing tonight than I was last night, but I'm still not quite ready. Is it all right?"

Buckskin grinned. "Sure, it's all right. Only thing, this is going to be a record for me. Spending two nights in bed with the same lovely lady and not making love to her."

Sara Jane whirled her long brown hair around from her back so most of it covered her breasts. "I hate to make you establish a new record like that, but at least I'd have a place in your record book." She leaned over and kissed his lips. "I suppose that

I could make an exception and take care of your needs one time tonight."

Buckskin smiled and kissed her nose, then bent and kissed both her breasts through the hair and her dress.

"Fine, lady. One time would be great, then we both can get some sleep."

She nodded as he unbuttoned her dress down the front and she unbuttoned his vest and shirt.

The moment he had her breasts free and bare, he bent and kissed them a dozen times, winding up with licking her nipples that had grown in size and stood proud and tall with hot new blood.

Sara Jane had been petting the growing bulge at his crotch. She soon had the buttons undone and pulled out his pink and purple hardness.

"My, what a dandy," Buckskin said. "Reminds me of someone else a long time ago."

"Don't tell me about it, Lee Buckskin Morgan. I want you to demonstrate."

She had him naked a few minutes later and pulled off her silk bloomers and tossed them on the floor. "I bought those at that fancy women's shop just so I could take them off for you," she said. "Did it work?"

"Worked well for me," he said. "That must mean you want to be on top."

"Oh, yes!" She squealed in delight as she pushed on top of his long, lean, muscular body. She lay there a moment, reveling in her position, then pushed higher so she could dangle one breast into his mouth.

"Now there's what I'd call the ideal dessert after a fine supper," he said, then gulped her into his mouth and chewed tenderly.

"Buckskin, you know that makes me go wild. Some girls said they hardly felt it when a man touched their breasts, but it just jolts me into ecstasy. Once you start to kiss me up there I'm gone and done for. When your mouth gets around one of my titties, I'd just as soon rape you as say howdy."

Sweat popped out on her forehead, and she groaned.

"Morgan, you tease, do me quick. Stick me with that long rake handle you got down there between your legs and don't listen if I say you're in deep enough. I don't care if you push all the way through me."

Buckskin caught her by her hips, lifted her whole body off him, moved her down and told her to direct things. She caught his erection and angled him upward. Then he let her down gently, and when he felt his erection penetrate her, he let her fall down all at once. She crashed into him pelvis first, and a gasp of wonder and amazement came from Sara Jane.

Her eyes were wide, and she started breathing like an old steam engine.

"Glory, James was a good lover, but he never thought of nothing like this. Glory be, but that is fine."

She grinned and tried to reach up to kiss his lips, but his face was too far away. She settled for nibbling at his nipple and then humping her hips upward and back down on his tool with a slow rhythm that got them both sweating and panting.

For the first time they worked up together, and almost at the same moment they both blasted each other with their climaxes.

They shouted and panted and humped and vibrated. Then both gulped in deep breaths to replenish their systems and fell together still gasping for breath, spent and delighted.

Ten minutes later they lay side by side. She put one hand on his chest and played with his black hair.

"What do we do tomorrow?" she asked.

"I could go see the sheriff, but somehow I'm not too set on that. The marshal at San Carlos Wells gave me the idea that the sheriff here wasn't the best lawman in the world. We're interested in the judge, whoever he is. If he's a real judge he could be in cahoots with a crooked sheriff. So, not a chance I'm going to check in with the sheriff.

"So we work the saloons, the general store, places where the bastards would probably shop if they lived here."

"Just how big is Phoenix? It's way bigger than San Carlos Wells."

"I heard that the town has something like five thousand people in it now. That means it's going to be a lot harder to find them than in a smaller place. But the basics still remain. They have to eat and sleep—and probably drink and gamble somewhere. A pair like Something Smith and Pointer would probably be easiest to find among the drinkers and gamblers."

The next morning they had breakfast at the hotel, then Buckskin started making the rounds of the saloons that opened early. He found three, and two of the barkeeps knew about Something Smith.

"Hell, yes, I know Something Smith. He's kind of a local celebrity. He's wanted in six states and even right here in Phoenix, but the lawmen can't find him. He's slippery, but just between you and me, I think he drops off some spare gold coins at the sheriff's office so they leave him alone."

"He buys off the sheriff?"

"Hell, nothing new about that. Been going on for years around here. The law ain't what it should be in most of the Arizona Territory, and when it comes to the local sheriff, it don't mean much at all.

"Something Smith been around lately?"

The apron started wiping a beer mug that was already clean and looked up and down his bar. "Hell, don't see him around right now. You look too much like a lawman or at least a bounty hunter for me to tell you much at all.

"A barkeep got to talking about two months ago, and when some bounty hunter crossed six-guns with Something Smith, they carted the varmint off to boot hill. The bounty hunter, not Something.

"Something Smith then had a quiet conversation with that barkeep the same afternoon. Didn't kill him, but he did put a .45 slug right through one of the gent's balls. He's alive, but he sure as hell ain't bothering the girls up on the second floor much. Used to be a real cock hound, but now he's just trying to heal up before he tries out his one-barreled pecker to see if he's got any grape shot left."

Buckskin sipped at his beer and laughed. "Yes, life does have its complications. You don't need to say nothing about this little talk to Mr. Smith. I still got two loads in my double barrel and I'd like to keep it that way."

The next barkeep also knew of Smith. "Yep, he's in and out of here now and then. Drinks moderately, gambles a little and uses the girls upstairs, but he never gets loud or causes any trouble. He's a perfect gent around this saloon."

The third drinking emporium had just opened, and the bartender was busy getting everything ready. He ignored Buckskin's query about Something Smith. When Morgan asked the question again, the apron came boiling down the bar and pointed a sawed-off shotgun at him.

"Get out of here. I don't talk about my customers. Especially I don't talk about Something Smith. Get the hell out of here before I cut you in half with this. I can claim you tried to rob me."

Buckskin backed toward the door, turned around and hurried out. He hated having a double-barreled sawed-off shotgun pointing at him more than anything else in this world.

It was only ten in the morning, and the rest of the watering holes wouldn't be open until noon. He went back to the hotel room and found Sara Jane up and dressed. It was one of the new outfits and she looked delicious. She had done up her hair in a big bun at the back of her neck.

"Like it?" she asked.

"Hate it. I like the dress, but I like to see your hair free and flowing around your bare breasts."

She kissed him quickly and looked up, her brown eyes giving him the signal that this was only a one kiss deal.

"I had an idea. I hear that this town has a good newspaper. The editor might know more about Something Smith than anyone else. Let's go down and talk to him or at least look through back issues."

"Great idea." He told her about his talk with the barkeeps.

"That last one sounded like he was afraid of Something Smith. I don't understand how he has everyone fooled. He's nothing more than a bully with a fast gun."

"For a lot of people that's a bad combination. Let's see what the editor has to say."

They walked into the newspaper office, and Buckskin grinned at the smell. It was a unique combination of the odor of newsprint and oil-based ink used in printing. No matter what newspaper office he entered, the smell was exactly the same. If he was blindfolded and had cotton stuffed in his ears he'd still recognize that particular, unmistakable smell.

A young woman sat at an office desk just beyond the front counter, working on a galley proof.

"I beg your pardon, miss, but is the editor here?" Buckskin asked.

"Just a minute," the woman said, not looking up and concentrating on the proof in front of her. She made a correction, initialed the bottom of the long strip of newsprint and stood.

"Now, what was it you wanted?"

She was maybe 25, taller than Buckskin had expected, with a big busted yet slender figure and with a shock of strawberry-blonde hair cascading down to her shoulders. Her face was long and beautiful with huge blue eyes and heavy lashes and brows.

"We were hoping to talk to the editor. Is he in?" Sara Jane asked.

The woman smiled, and Buckskin felt his knees weaken. Her smile was magnificent, something you wish you could preserve with a photograph.

"The editor certainly is in. That's me, G.J. Hazleton. My friends call me Ginger. The G.J. is for business purposes."

"Ginger, I'm Buckskin Morgan and this lady is Sara Jane Nelson. Her husband was killed by Something Smith and his gang less than a week ago, and we're here to find out all we can about the gang."

Ginger looked at Sara Jane, and a small worry line etched into her creamy forehead. "Oh, I'm so sorry. Smith is an outlaw, an animal who should be jailed or shot down—and the sooner the better."

"Then you know about him? Maybe where he lives?" Sara Jane asked. "When I find him, I'm going to kill him."

Ginger closed her eyes and slowly shook her head. "Mrs. Nelson, you don't know what you're saying. Something Smith has been terrorizing this part of Arizona Territory for three years. There's been talk that he lives here in Phoenix and does his dirty work in the rest of the territory. There's also talk that he has the protection of our illustrious county sheriff, Douglas Abady."

"You must write a lot of stories about Something Smith," Buckskin said.

The lady laughed without humor and shook her head. "Not that you could count. Something Smith and the sheriff are both on my list of save-your-life stories. I don't touch either one of them."

"But you say he's a crooked sheriff . . ." Sara Jane began.

"Yes, that's right." Ginger came up to the counter and put the marked-up proof beside the current edition of the paper. "Something Smith is a dangerous outlaw, and Sheriff Abady should be ridden out of the county on a cactus rail. I can't do a thing about either one."

"I don't understand," Buckskin said. "What happened to the power of the press?"

"It died in Arizona. A little paper in a town to the south took off on Something Smith after he'd shot down an unarmed man in a saloon down there. Called for Smith to be shot on sight. The night after the paper came out, the newspaper's office building burned to the ground with the editor inside. After the fire they couldn't tell if he'd been beaten to death, shot down or died when he was trapped in the fire. They did decide that the fire had started at both the front and the back doors with large quantities of kerosene."

"I can understand your reluctance," Buckskin said. He watched her and found her looking at him. She smiled and looked away.

"Ginger, there's another piece of the puzzle. The killers said they had to do the job just as the judge told them to. Any idea who they might have been referring to?"

Ginger's smile faded. Her eyes turned cold, and she took a step back. "No, no idea at all. I'm busy now, getting ready to close the front page. Sorry I can't help you. Thanks for stopping by."

She turned and walked through the swinging door into the back shop.

Buckskin and Sara Jane went out the front door to the boardwalk. Sara Jane's eyes were shooting off sparks.

"Did you see her? She froze up the minute you mentioned the judge. She knows something about who he is. I'd bet my ranch she knows who the judge is. We've got to find a way to make her tell us."

Chapter Six

The office was one of the best in Phoenix. It had soft wall-to-wall carpeting on the floor, two fancy lamps on special stands, thick, expensive drapes over the one window and original oil paintings on three of the walls which were paneled in beautifully grained walnut. Above the paneling, the walls and ceiling were papered with a light brown pattern.

The man sitting behind the big desk remained in the shadows. One of the lamps was situated so it shone in the eyes of the two men who stood ramrod stiff in front of the wide cherrywood desk. The top of it had been polished to a sheen, and only one folder lay there.

Both standing men waited patiently for the one sitting to speak. One of the men was Something Smith. He was clean-shaven, wore dandified town clothes and smelled of rose water and bay rum shaving lotion. His shock of white hair had been carefully cut around his neck and ears and combed neatly.

The other man was Will Pointer, a head shorter than Smith, with sunken dark eyes, a three day growth of beard and clothes that could have been the same ones he wore when he helped kill James Nelson almost a week ago. He chewed tobacco, and a thin brown line ran down from the corner of his mouth. He wiped it away with his dirty left sleeve, and it was obvious that he wanted a place to spit.

The man in the shadows cleared his throat.

"What happened in San Carlos Wells?"

"Don't know what you mean, sir," Smith said.

"Pointer, did you do it?" the hidden man asked in a booming voice that jolted Pointer half a step back.

"No, sir, not me. Something and me rode right on through. Larson said he had a little woman he had to see when we last talked to him. We couldn't of done nothing in that town."

"You won't converse with Larson anymore. Somebody shot him in the heart with a small caliber handgun."

"Dead?" Smith asked.

"Extremely dead, Mr. Smith. Most men die who get shot through the heart. No great loss, gentlemen. Larson was a stupid man, and we don't have any room for his kind in this operation. What I'm wondering is if he said anything that might tie him to you or to me. We have to be on the watch for that sort of small mistake. Those are the kind of mistakes that lead to men like you stretching a hemp rope after a six foot drop."

"He didn't say what he was going to do there beside see that little poon girl," Something Smith said. "Don't see why you're getting so hot with us about it."

The man in the shadows sighed and mumbled a few words, then lifted his voice. "No, Smith, you wouldn't see. He was working for me, damn it. He was on a job most important to me. If he said the wrong thing, this whole project could be in jeopardy. If so, both you and Mr. Pointer here would also be in extreme danger. Now do you understand?"

Something Smith scowled back at his boss. "Just you remember that this extreme danger problem is a two-way street. If we're in danger then so are you. Damn, you told us not to kill the woman, so we didn't. You told us she'd just faint and fall away, probably go back East somewhere. We did like we was told. We don't like to be rawhided about it up one side and down the damn other side."

"Yes, yes, yes, Mr. Smith. I understand. Don't get so upset. I am being a little overcautious in this situation. I'm concerned because this project is so important to me and to you as well. When I make money, you make money. Now, go out and have a good time. You've earned it. I'll be in touch with you for more work."

Something Smith and Pointer left by a back door in the alley. They made sure no one saw them come out the door and then hurried up the alley to Main.

"What's he getting so all-fired mad about?" Pointer asked. "Shit, we done exactly what he told us to do."

"He's jumpy. This project he's on must be bigger than we thought. We might stand to profit if it all works out. He said if he made money, then we made money."

"So let's spend some of this green money we got in our pockets," Pointer said. "I'm about set for a good drinking spree and then find me a little woman to spread her legs for me all night."

Something Smith grinned. "Think you're about right, and this time we won't have to tie the heifer's hand and foot to get at the good stuff!"

Further down the street Buckskin and Sara Jane stood outside the newspaper office talking. They had just left the editor, and Sara Jane was suspicious.

"I still think she knows more about the judge than she told us. Why don't we barge back in there and demand that she tell us?"

"Sara Jane, you know more about women than that. Push that lady and she will clam up like a steel trap. Let me talk to her later. Maybe we rattled her nice, warm, little niche in Phoenix and she'll do some asking on her own.

"Why don't we have something to eat and do some planning? I've been thinking what I'd do if I was in this town after making some easy money. I'd gamble some. But first I'd need a place to stay. If they live here all the time, they must have a regular place."

"The likes of them won't do the cooking and dishwashing," Sara Jane said. "They'd live in a hotel or in a rooming house."

"A hotel would be too expensive for a home base. Let's find out how many boarding houses there are in town. It's a long chance, but it might pay off."

Sara Jane shook her head as they walked down the street. "Too many boarding houses. In a town this size there must be thirty or forty at least. Your idea about the saloons and whorehouses is better to help us find Something Smith fast. Of course, there's not much I can do to help you there."

"Which means we eat something and I get back to saloon crawling. Half a beer in each of twenty saloons and I might not be in such good shape myself."

"Then you'll just have to pretend to drink."

They ate at a café, and then Sara Jane excused herself. "I have an important place to go. I saw this dress store a while back, and there's a dress in the window that . . . . Well, you go try to find our friends. I'm going to spend some of this money I hoarded for the past three years."

Every saloon Buckskin went in that afternoon had a barkeep who remembered Something Smith. Two of the men wouldn't say a word about Smith. One asked him to leave and wouldn't sell him a beer. The next one nodded grimly when asked about Smith.

"Damn right I know him. The big bastard owes me thirty dollars, and I don't have a prayer of collecting it. He smashed one of my big mirrors behind the bar here. I ain't seen him since and doubt if he'll ever come in here again. I thought of going to the sheriff, but the damn sheriff is afraid of Smith, just like about half the men in this town."

"What does he do for a living?"

"Don't know. Doesn't work for any of the big cattle outfits. Don't think he has a regular job here in town. Might be he robs banks for all I know."

In the next saloon, Buckskin checked out every man in the place before he talked to the barkeep. There was one man with white hair, but he had to be pushing the far side of 70. The place was one of the largest Buckskin had been in.

The barkeep was close-mouthed but finally did talk.

"Sure, I know Something Smith. He's been in town longer than I have. I got no fight with him. He never has been in any trouble in here while I been on duty. He's not here right now."

Buckskin thanked him and started to leave. "Oh, one more question. I'm hunting a man called the judge. You know where I could find him? Not sure of the gent's name. Is he a municipal or county judge of some kind?"

The barman wiped at the counter where it was already clean and shrugged. "Hey, you got me. We don't have no judge in this town far as I know. One comes through about twice a year or so. Best I can do."

Buckskin thanked the apron and took a pull on his beer. A man probably in his fifties stood down the bar staring into an empty beer mug. He slid it toward Buckskin who caught it before it crashed into his own glass mug.

The old-timer guffawed. "Almost got you, sonny," he said. When Buckskin didn't react with anger, the man slid up the bar a few spaces. "Could you see yur way clear to setting up a beer for me, mister? You look like you been lucky at the cards."

"I'm not a gambler, but I reckon I can pop for a dime." Buckskin reached in his pocket, pulled out a dime and spun it down the polished counter to the apron. "Draw one," Buckskin said. When the frothing beer mug came, Buckskin passed it on to the old-timer.

"Bless you, mister. You're a kind man."

"Okay, Ollie, that's the last one today," the barkeep said with a touch of anger. "You go mooch somewhere else."

Buckskin nodded and left the drinking parlor. He was hearing the same thing over and over about Something Smith. No sense duplicating his efforts. He'd have to check on the saloons when they got roaring later tonight and hope that he could track down Smith. He turned toward the hotel.

Ollie, the old-timer who had cadged the drink off Buckskin, downed the brew in record time, hurried out of the saloon and followed his benefactor. He had a glint in his eye as he kept well back, but he trailed the big man in the brown vest to the Salt River Hotel. Ollie ran down the boardwalk and got to the door just in time to see the big man head for the hotel desk.

Ollie walked into the hotel far enough to spot the box the room clerk reached into when the man asked for his key. Second row, third box from the left side. He knew that key case. Two years before he had worked in this hotel. The numbers on the second floor began with 210, so the tall one in the brown leather vest resided in room 212.

Ollie thought about getting the man's name, but he had enough information. No sense in getting in trouble here. He hurried out of the hotel just before the room clerk headed for him. He had plenty, and it should be worth more than a dollar. As he walked, he tried to divide a dollar into ten cent beers but couldn't come up with the number.

He headed up an alley behind Main Street to a staircase that went to the second floor. He looked both ways, then hurried up the steps and through a door without knocking. Inside he paced down the familiar hallway to a big door and knocked.

Nothing happened. He knocked again, and after a long pause the door opened a crack.

A voice rasped at him, and Ollie shied back a step.

"You? What the hell you want, old-timer?"

"I've got some information you might be interested in."

"Not hardly, Ollie. What would an old drunk like you know?"

"Know there's a man in town looking through the saloons and asking a hell of a lot of questions about Something Smith. I seen him this morning, then again this afternoon. He asks the same questions."

"So? Maybe he's kin, or he owes Smith money," the man said through the narrow crack in the door.

"Maybe. He could be a lawman or a bounty hunter. Just kind of had that look. Then he asked another question. He asked the barkeep who the judge was and where he could find him."

The door jolted open a foot, and the man in a dark suit and full beard scowled, removed a half-smoked cigar from his mouth and glared at Ollie.

"You sure about that, Ollie? You wouldn't say that to your old friend just to get a handout, would you?"

"Hell, no. I know what's what around this town. I also know where the gent is staying and his room number."

"No name?"

"I ain't as good as I used to be. No name. But the room number at the Salt River Hotel is two-one-two."

The bearded man's hand flashed out and caught around Ollie's throat. "You damn sure you ain't lying to me, old man? This could be important to me."

Ollie's eyes went wild, and he wheezed as he tried to breathe.

"You lying to me, Ollie?"

The bearded man loosened his grip, and Ollie wheezed and blinked back tears as he got his breath.

"Damn, why you do that? I never lie to you. You know that. Damn, this is worth at least a fiver."

The man in the black suit nodded. He went back to his desk, scribbled a note and gave it to Ollie.

"Here's a ten dollar tab for you at the Salt Saloon. You give it to the apron there and he'll take care of you. Just don't drink it all up in one night."

Ollie looked at the note but couldn't read it. His eyes went bad two years ago, and he hadn't been able to read good since. He grinned.

"Yes sir, yes sir! I sure as hell won't drink it all up in one night." Ollie turned and hurried down the hallway to the stairs, the note held tightly in his hand.

The bearded man in the black suit went back to his office and tapped on the door that led to the outer area. A moment later a man came in. He wore a town suit, was clean-shaven and had a six-gun slung low on his right hip. His eyes were dark, and he was a thinly built five-feet-ten.

"Yeah, boss?"

"Small matter for you to take care of tonight. Old Ollie is talking too much. You'll find him at the Salt Saloon. Late tonight Ollie has a fatal fall in the alley behind the saloon. He went to the outhouse and fell and hit his head. Make it look good and be careful."

The man nodded, adjusted his gun belt and looked at his employer. "Anything else?"

"Yes, but later, after this small problem is taken care of. Oh, this afternoon give the room clerk at the Salt River Hotel two dollars and find out who is registered in room 212."

The man bobbed his head and left the room.

The big man in the black suit and full black beard sat down behind his desk and peaked his fingers together as he thought through the situation. All was moving along nicely. Tomorrow was another big step, then he would be in the driver's seat. Not a hell of a lot could be done to stop him after tomorrow.

He relit the cigar and puffed on it until he made a perfect smoke ring that floated almost to the ceiling. As he watched it rise, he went over his plans again. Yes, tomorrow was the key. Without that he had nothing. With it he had what could be a million dollars. He had waited long enough. It was about time that the fates smiled on him.

He grunted. Better that they smile on him than on a nobody named James Nelson.

Chapter Seven

Lee Buckskin Morgan worked the rest of the saloons in Phoenix that afternoon but turned up nothing new. He did let a lot of people know that he was looking for Something Smith, and that in itself could be productive.

With that in mind, Buckskin went back to the Salt River Hotel and checked for a vacant room. Number 216 across the hall was not occupied. He used the same key to open it he used on his old room and moved all of his and Sara Jane's things into the new room.

He didn't tell the desk clerk about this. It might be prudent to let others think he was staying in 212 and be somewhere else.

After one final check of the new quarters, Buckskin left the hotel and angled down the boardwalk toward Maud's Café, where he was supposed to meet Sara Jane for supper. He was halfway there when a man dressed like a towner came screaming out of an alley across the street, bellowing and braying in total panic.

By the time Buckskin crossed the street and got to the man, he had led a dozen men and women up the alley. The people huddled around a body on the ground next to some trash boxes.

Buckskin moved up closer so he could see who it was. At first he didn't recognize the small man lying on his side in the dirt and garbage. A better look helped Buckskin make the connection.

The man was Ollie, the moocher Buckskin had bought a beer for that morning. He looked dead.

"Just the way I found him, honest," the still frightened man told them. "He was there, and I didn't see him because I was carrying a box. Then I stumbled over him. I sprawled on the ground right on top of him, his dead eyes looked at me, and I ran like crazy."

Sheriff Abady came pushing through the crowd that had grown to more than 30.

"Make way there. Let me see what this is all about. A body, somebody said."

The people parted for the lawman who knelt down beside the corpse. "Be damned if it isn't old Ollie. Somebody get tired of him stealing his drink and shot the old fart?"

"Don't see no bullet holes," one of the men in the crowd said.

The sheriff rolled Ollie over on his back. A bloody patch four inches long showed on his forehead and down across one eye.

"Looks like he was drunk as usual, fell and hit his head and bashed in his own brains. I been telling him to ease off on the booze."

"Most drunks are so relaxed that they don't hurt themselves when they fall," another voice said from the crowd.

"Looks like old Ollie sure as hell did." The sheriff put his finger to Ollie's forehead, then to his throat searching for some sign of pulse. "This man is stone dead. Wilbur, you go fetch the undertaker so we can get him out of here."

"Mighty quick judgment on cause of death," Buckskin said. "Looks like that wound could have come from a pistol whipping or a heavy rock or a two-by-four. How do you know it came from a fall, Sheriff?"

"Who the hell are you, mister?"

Buckskin stepped forward. "Don't you have a coroner in this county to judge things like this?"

"Hell, yes. Dr. Chambers does it if there's any question. I say there's no question here. Doc don't have time to fool with riffraff like old Ollie here. He was nothing but a drunk."

"I'd say there's a lot of questions about what caused Ollie's death, Sheriff," Buckskin continued. "That smash on the side of the head is in the wrong place for a man falling down. Besides, look at those red bruise marks on Ollie's throat.

"Those are the kind of marks left when a person is strangled to death. If I was you, Sheriff, I'd want to be sure about those bruises before you bury old Ollie. My money says that any doctor worth his pills would agree with me."

"Yeah, now I peg you. New man in town asking a lot of questions. Don't much cotton to outsiders butting into my business. Best if you just mosey on out of here before I run you into my jail as a common drunk."

The sheriff turned. "You and you, get over here and carry old Ollie down to the undertaker. He's gonna take all day to get here. Don't want this kind of trash littering the alley. Come on, pick him up and let's move."

Buckskin watched the men carry the body down the alley toward the undertaker's place. Old Ollie did not die by hitting his head. Somebody slammed him with the butt of a six-gun, then choked him to death. Why would anyone want to kill old Ollie?

Supper at the café was subdued. They were making no progress. They had no lines on Something Smith or the judge and no real prospects.

"What are we going to do?" Sara Jane said, reaching across the table for his hand. "I can't just go back to the ranch and pretend that it's all settled and that I can go on like before, only now with a hired man. I'd always wonder."

"It's going to take more time than I figured. This is a big place. They say now the town has more than seven thousand people here. A man could hide away here for years."

"Something Smith isn't the kind to hide."

"You're right. Tonight I'm going to cruise through as many saloons as I can, hoping to spot him. With that white hair he won't be hard to find if he's out on the town."

"What am I supposed to do? Sit in the hotel and twiddle my thumbs?"

"You could buy another new dress, but the store will be closed."

"Don't tease me. I'm in no mood. I want to do something."

"Sara Jane, I know you do, and you've been a big help already. But you can't go saloon prospecting with me. Find a book or a magazine and settle down for a read."

"I guess I'll have to. That or take a nap before I go to bed." She smiled. "You'll be back early tonight? I just thought that we might . . . you know."

Buckskin grinned. "With that kind of an invitation I'll make it a point not to stay out too late. But right now it's important to find Smith and get some track on what he's doing, maybe even where he lives.

"Tomorrow we can work on boarding houses for both Smith and Pointer. My guess is that they have separate boarding houses. It's the simplest way for a bachelor to get a bed and some food."

They finished fresh baked apple pie piled with whipped cream, then left the eatery. Sara Jane motioned with one hand.

"The millinery shop is still open. I'll stop by there before I go back to the hotel."

He nodded, not really hearing her. She slipped away and moved down the boardwalk, her hips showing their gentle swaying through the new dress. His mind was on his work. Find Something Smith. He wasn't sure why it was so important. He wasn't being hired to find the man; in fact, he had no business mixing in. But a woman had been brutalized and her husband tortured and killed, and Lee Buckskin Morgan didn't like it. Justice, at least a little bit of frontier justice, had to be done in this case.

He checked the first saloon, making a sweeping look around the tables and the bar. Buckskin saw no one who could remotely be Something Smith. Pointer would be harder to identify, since he had no good description of him.

The second and third saloons also yielded nothing. Maybe the pair had already hit the stairways up to the cribs. If so, he might not see them all night.

He had just stepped up on the boardwalk to go to the next saloon, when he caught sight of a light in the newspaper office. Then it went out, and someone came through the front door.

"Oh, Miss Hazleton. Looks like you're closing up for the night."

She frowned as she tried to place him, then she brightened. "Yes, Mr. Morgan. Sorry I didn't recognize you right away. Your voice was what gave you away. It's low and solid, very distinctive. Yes, I'm about worked out." She hesitated. "I did want to talk to you again."

"Would now be a good time?" he asked.

Ginger Hazleton hesitated. She looked back at the dark building. "Yes, Mr. Morgan, I think this would be a good time, if I'm not taking you away from some important business."

Buckskin chuckled. "Nothing I've done all day could be pegged as important. Could I buy you a cup of coffee?"

"You could, but mine is better than they serve in town. Let's go back inside, and I'll brew us up some coffee and we can have our talk."

"Fine by me. I'm partial to good coffee after drinking my own so many times."

She smiled, returned to the office door, unlocked it, then stepped inside. He followed her. She lit a lamp that had been left near the front door and motioned to him.

"The coffee is in back upstairs. This way."

Upstairs turned out to be her living quarters. She led him into a living room, and he saw a kitchen off to one side and a closed door to what must be a bedroom.

Ginger led him to the kitchen where she lit a second lamp and checked a small cast-iron stove. Ginger built a fire as she began to talk.

"I've been doing some more probing around town, questioning people I know I can trust and trying to find out who the judge really is. Most of the people I talk to have heard of him, but they just haven't been able to pin him down. I've had hints and clues here and there and might be on the right track."

"I think the judge is behind the killing. What I can't figure out is why," Buckskin said. "The spread James Nelson had was marginal. It might be able to support four hundred head of stock. That's on a good year. That means there could be no more than fifty head that would be ready for market in any one year. That's not enough cash money to keep a spread running even if it's a homestead ranch."

"That's bothered me, too," Ginger said. She lit the fire she had set. It burned up brightly in the small kindling, then caught heavier split wood.

"Why send three men to kill one rancher on a small place seventy-five miles away in the foothills? It just doesn't make sense."

Ginger measured out some ground coffee from a tightly sealed jar, added water to a coffeepot and put it on the range top.

"We don't have all the facts," Buckskin said. "There has to be a good reason to kill Nelson. When we know what the reason is, we'll probably have the judge unmasked."

"The problem is to figure out the reason," Ginger said. "Everything I've heard has led nowhere."

Buckskin liked to watch the way she moved. She was confident and incisive, her medium long blonde hair swinging around her shoulders as she made the fire. Now she set out cups and saucers on a small kitchen table that had a white linen cloth over it. He also appreciated the tight way her breasts pushed against her cream-colored blouse. It was buttoned securely all the way to her chin, and the sleeves came down to her wrists.

"I was hoping to get information out of Something Smith, but now I'm not even sure if I can find him," Buckskin said. "Smith could end up the same way that old Ollie did this afternoon."

"You heard about that?"

"I saw him in the alley. Sheriff said it was an accident. I told him it couldn't have been. There were bruises on his throat where someone had strangled him."

Ginger grinned. "I bet that made a hit with our sheriff. Mr. Abady doesn't like to be contradicted or corrected. He's always right." She came over and sat across from him at the small table.

"I'm really glad I bumped into you tonight. I . . . I don't like to drink coffee alone."

"Neither do I."

"This nice lady, Mrs. Nelson. How did you happen to get the job of helping her on her mission?"

He told her about finding her after the slaughter.

"You might say I volunteered. I hate to see somebody pounded into the dirt. Time to take a stand, I guess."

"That's noble of you, Mr. Morgan."

"Please, call me Buckskin."

She smiled, and her soft blue eyes danced. "I will, Buckskin, if you'll call me Ginger."

"For Virginia?"

"Yes, but that's so formal and stiff. I like Ginger better."

The coffee boiled, and she went to check on the fire. He also stood, and when she turned, she was right in front of him, almost touching. She hesitated.

He reached out and caught her shoulders, and she looked up at him. Slowly he brought his head down toward hers. There was plenty of time for her to protest or back away. She did neither and lifted her head a little until their lips met. It was a short, sweet kiss, and she pulled back first.

"Surprises are fun," she said, her smile growing.

"No surprise this time," Buckskin said. He moved to her lips again, and his arms went around her, pulling her gently against him until her breasts flattened against his chest.

Her arms crept around him, and the kiss lasted much longer this time. At last she eased away, and he let her go.

"My, oh my, but that was nice."

"Just about perfect," Buckskin said.

Ginger put two more narrow splits of wood into the fire and looked over at him.

"Are you in the habit of kissing women who ask you in for a cup of coffee?"

Buckskin laughed softly and nodded. "Are you in the habit of inviting virtual strangers into your apartment and then encouraging them to kiss you?"

They both grinned.

She waggled a finger at him. "Now settle down, Mr. Morgan."

"What happened to Buckskin."

"That was before you kissed me twice."

"That was before you *wanted* me to kiss you twice."

Ginger stared at him for a moment, eyes wide, surprise on her face. The surprise turned to a smile and a nod.

"You're right, but I'll never admit it. I think the coffee is ready." She brought back the pot of coffee and poured their cups full, then set the pot on the back part of the store to keep warm without any more boiling.

She looked up at him, blonde hair framing her pretty face. "So now?"

"Now we talk about how to find the judge."

She stared at him, her face open and vulnerable. "I think I talked that out. I want to talk about you. Where do you come from?"

"All over the west. I began up in Idaho on a horse ranch my father ran."

"But you're not a rancher now?"

"No. I move around a lot."

"A saddle tramp?"

"No, I don't like working cattle."

"You're a lawman?"

He grinned. "Not really, but I've seen some towns where I'd like to take over and hang a few people."

"I can understand that. You're not an outlaw. Are you independently wealthy?"

"Sure, just me and my millions in that Boise bank."

"Seriously, Buckskin."

"Seriously I do some work as a detective, here and there. I sometimes have an address in San Francisco where people write to me who need help."

"Help like Mrs. Nelson?"

"The same."

"But she didn't write to you?"

"No."

They sipped their coffee, and Buckskin felt the need to move on. When he stood up, she came to her feet and led the way back down the steps to the front door. Before he reached for the knob, she stretched up and touched his lips with hers, so gently that he wasn't sure they had met. An electric charge sparked between them, and she let out a little gasp.

Then she was in his arms, and the kiss was full and strong and she pushed against him from chest to knee.

He came away from her first.

"Ginger, I think it's time for me to get back on my job. I'm trying to spot Something Smith in a saloon."

She looked at the closed door, still holding him against her.

"You really have to go?"

"I . . . I think it might be best. I like your kisses too much." He undid her hands from behind him, bent and kissed her forehead, then reached for the doorknob.

"I'll need to let you out," she said.

She caught his shirt front and held on to him.

"You know I don't want you to go," she said, her voice husky with a slight tremble in it.

"I know. Another few kisses and I'd be here all night. I promised myself I'd run this skunk out of his hole, so I'm doing it. Another time?"

She reached up and kissed his lips gently. "Yes, Buckskin Morgan, another day when we both have time."

She unlocked the front door and let him out. He smiled at her in the gloom of the unlighted front door, then walked away. Ginger closed and locked the door, then leaned against it for more than a minute, dreaming about what might have been.

Chapter Eight

For two more hours, Buckskin prowled the lowlife saloons in Phoenix. He lost count of how many he visited. Nowhere did he find Something Smith. He finished his beer in the last saloon and pushed through the swinging doors to the street. The Salt River Hotel was only a half block away. Good.

As soon as he walked in the front door, he heard a shout and Sara Jane Nelson stormed up to him, her eyes flashing, her arms akimbo, her face blushing furiously.

"Where have you been? Why did you move us out of our room? I went up there, and there's nothing in it at all. Did somebody rob us, or did you move our things? Tell me what's going on here."

He caught her arm, waved at the desk clerk who had been trying to listen to what Sara Jane said, and guided her up the steps.

Patiently he explained why he had moved their things to a different room and hadn't told the room clerk.

By the time they got to room 216 and slipped inside, Sara Jane had calmed down.

"Sorry I blew up down there, but I've been sitting in that damned lobby for three hours waiting for you to show up." She reached up and kissed his lips. "Now you might at least admit that you should have warned me about moving to a new room, and then I'll let you rub my back. It's aching."

They undressed, and he rubbed her back. Then he rubbed her front and things got serious. They made love once, gently and slowly, with glorious results.

As they lay in each other's arms afterwards, she kissed his chest then looked up at him. "You any ideas of settling down? I know where there's a small ranch that needs a foreman. If the gent played his cards right he might just get lucky and hitch up in double harness with the widow who owns the place. Nothing I want you to talk about now. You just consider the idea and the benefits that go along with the deal." She took his hand and put it over one of her breasts.

"You just think about that double teaming, Lee Buckskin Morgan. Way I look at it, you got nothing better to do, and it could be a right nice place to settle down."

Buckskin nodded, kissed her breast and then moved away. "Yes, something to think about. Now we better get some sleep."

Sometime later that same night, a blast nearly shook them out of their bed.

"What the hell?" Buckskin said, jolting upright.

Sara Jane stared up at him only half-awake. "Did I hear something?"

"A blast, a big one and nearby." He stepped out of the bed naked and went to the door. He turned the key in the lock and edged the door open half an inch.

A gush of smoke surged into the room, and he closed the door.

"Dynamite blast just outside somewhere. I can tell by the smell of the smoke."

He tried the door again, but this time no smoke came in. He peered through the inch wide slot. The hall was still filled with smoke, but now it was thin enough to see through. Doors had opened along the hallway. Down a ways and across, he could see their old room, 212.

Where the door used to be was only a gaping hole. Smashed and splintered pieces of the door littered the hallway. He closed their door softly and locked it, then turned the key halfway around, leaving it in the lock so no other key could unlock the door. He pushed a straight chair under the doorknob and braced it on its back legs.

"Our old room had a visitor who left a bomb in it," Buckskin said. "Could have thrown it through the door or through the window. Damn lucky we weren't sleeping in there tonight or both of us would be deader than last week's roast beef."

Sara Jane shuddered, her hands covering her face. She swayed toward him, and he caught her.

"No danger now. We'll keep moving around nights so they don't know where we're staying. Could even try another hotel. I've been this route before. It seems we must be making the judge and his bully boys nervous. Why else would they try to blow our bodies into mincemeat?"

"They're trying to kill us, really trying to kill us," Sara Jane whispered, her voice a concentrated tremble. "I've never had anyone sneak around and try to actually end my life before. It's terrible. It's so scary that I'm shivering. How could anyone do something like that?"

Tears came then, and she cried quietly. He held her, and slowly she worked her way out of it.

"Sara Jane, it's going to be all right. I'll make sure of that. Now let's get some sleep."

Buckskin eased Sara Jane back down on the bed and pulled the sheet up over them. He held her until she went back to sleep.

The next morning after breakfast, Sara Jane took a list of boarding houses she got from the desk clerk and started making the rounds. She really wasn't hoping to find where the two men lived, but at least it gave her something to do.

The room clerk had almost asked her something, then saw Buckskin coming and waved good-bye to her.

Buckskin stared hard at the room clerk who fidgeted, looked away, then back at him.

"Yes, Mr. Morgan. What can I do for you?"

"You can stop telling anyone who asks what room I'm using. You told someone it was two-twelve, and last night it got blown into bits. No, we weren't in it last night.

"You won't know what room we're using, and you don't want to know. If you tell anyone else, I'll slice off a strip of your skin from your scalp right down to your toes. Do we have an understanding, young man?"

"Yes, Mr. Morgan. I didn't tell no one, honest, but I'm not on the desk at night. I certainly won't tell a soul, Mr. Morgan, no sir, not me."

Morgan left the hotel, walked up the street and pushed into the saloon where he had bought the last mug of beer that old Ollie probably ever drank. The same barkeep was on duty.

Buckskin stared at him hard, and the apron held up his hands.

"Don't get on me, friend. I had nothing to do with it. You're riled because old Ollie got suddenly dead. Wasn't none of my doings."

"Then whose fault was it?"

"Probably old Ollie himself. Ollie was a snitch." A patron came in, and the apron served him a mug and the man went back to a table. When no one could hear, the barkeep went on.

"Old Ollie was a snitch. He heard things and sold the information to people. I figure he heard you asking me about Something Smith. Smith himself would be interested, and since Smith works for the judge, he'd be interested as well."

"But why not come after me, instead of Ollie?"

"He could tie it back to them. As I hear it somebody did come after you last night with some dynamite thrown through the hotel window. Hell, the story is all over town."

"They missed."

"Wrong room? You couldn't have lived through that."

"Wrong room. What I want to know is who the hell is this judge."

The apron looked around. "Damn it, keep your voice down. You never know who's listening. The judge has ears all over town, so he knows everything that goes on. If'n I was you, I'd be knee high on a good piece of horseflesh heading out of town."

"You're not me, friend. I'll see the judge six feet under or on the end of a strong hemp rope before I run away from him."

The barkeep lifted a mug of beer. "Damn but that would be great if somebody would. First you got to figure out just who the hell he is."

"Working on it," Buckskin said. He waved and left the saloon.

Down the street a block and a half, the judge sat behind his desk, glaring at a man who stood before him.

"When I give you a job to do, Ezra, I expect it to be done neatly, completely and with certainty. You fouled it up every which way. The worst part is you didn't kill this Buckskin Morgan."

The judge stood up and paced around the room. "Now he knows that somebody is after his hide. He'll be cautious as all hell now. He still has to be killed, and it's still your job. You have one more chance, Ezra. If you fail this time you might better get on the stage and just keep going until you're back East somewhere. Do I make myself perfectly clear, Ezra?"

"Yes, sir. But the night clerk assured me that the information was right. Morgan and the woman were both in that room, two-twelve. Everything worked fine. I swung the bomb down from the roof on a piece of rope so I couldn't miss."

"But you didn't kill him. Now get out of here and don't come back until this Buckskin Morgan is deader than your great-grandfather."

Ezra gave a curt nod and left the room quickly, his big Colt banging against his thigh as he moved.

The judge stared after Ezra for a moment. "Damned incompetents. I pay good money to people and all they do is make mistakes. That's bad for business." Ezra had left by the back door. Now the judge heard a familiar voice in the outer office. He opened the door and smiled when he saw who it was.

"Try Again, you old desert rat. It's good to see you. This is the day you get rich, Try Again."

The man he spoke to was an inch over five feet tall and had skin on his face and hands burned almost black by the sun and wind. His eyes squinted even in the best light as they had to do for years of prowling the desert hills looking for that one big strike—gold or silver. Try Again didn't care which.

He'd been through more than 50 different partners in his lifetime on the Arizona desert. Most had staked him to a donkey, a pack of food and enough water to take him to the next spring in the desert. For this grubstake he agreed to share on a 50/50 basis anything that he discovered.

Try Again's face broke into what he called a smile as he walked into the judge's office. He wore the same clothes he always did—two pairs of tattered pants tough enough to stand up to rough duty in the outback. His shirtsleeves had been cut off six inches from the cuffs because the cuffs had worn out.

Try Again figured like the Indians did. A blanket in the winter kept out the cold. A blanket in the summer kept out the heat.

He grinned and held out his hand. "This the day we close the deal?" he asked, his voice harsh and croaky from long disuse. No sense talking to the desert rocks or to a mule.

"Absolutely, Try Again. You have the map, and I have a paper for you to sign with a copy for yourself. Then we're in business."

"And the up front grubstake of double eagles?"

"Yes, twenty of them, just like I promised. Four hundred dollars. That's as much as a working man makes all year."

"More cash money than I've seen since I sold my house in Illinois thirty years ago. Where's the money?"

"Where's the map?"

"Oh, yeah, I got it, down on paper and in my head. Let's see the color of that gold."

The judge reached in a drawer and brought out a leather pouch about four inches deep. It weighed twenty ounces, well over a pound. The judge untied the leather drawstrings and opened the top of the pouch. He poured 20 gold double eagles on the polished desk top.

Try Again yelped in delight. "By damn, gold!" He grabbed as many as he could in one hand and held them up. Then he calmed down a little and stacked them up in fours on the desk and stood there looking down at the gold.

Slowly he reached in his pants pocket and pulled out a much-folded piece of paper. When he unfolded it and pushed it across the desk, the judge grabbed it and studied the crude map. He had one question about a landmark, then folded it and put it in his inside jacket pocket.

"Take the money, Try Again. It's time to look at our agreement." The judge pushed a paper across the desk, figuring that the old-timer couldn't read. "It's all there, just like we agreed to when we talked—the partnership and the fifty/fifty split of the profits."

Try Again stared down at the paper, then he nodded. "Where do I sign?"

"Right there," the judge said. "On that line where it says who discovered the strike. That's you."

"You're sure everything is in here we talked about?"

"Absolutely, Try Again. You read most of it, so you must know that."

"Well, yeah." The old man shrugged again and signed the document with a slow and careful hand. It was barely legible. When he finished writing, Try Again picked up the gold pieces one by one and counted them into the pouch. He put it on a string around his neck and dropped it under his shirt.

"Now, by damn, I'm going to buy me a bottle and go out in the country and get falling down drunk where nobody can steal my gold. Yes sirree, that's what I'm going to do."

Two blocks west of where the prospector signed the agreement, Sara Jane went up to another boarding house and knocked on the door. It was her fifth. So far she had been told they didn't rent to women at one place and that there was no vacancy the next. At the third place nobody was home.

She waited and then knocked again. Still no one came. Then she heard a window rattle above her and stepped back a few paces to look upward. A woman pushed her head and shoulders out the second story window.

"Yeah, you want something?" the woman asked.

"Wondering if you had a certain boarder here. I'm trying to find my uncle, Something Smith. He didn't tell me where he lived. Does he stay here?"

"Nope, got nobody by that name."

"He could be using another name—Willy Pointer. Is he here?"

"Never heard of that name either. Best you try somewhere else. I don't have time to chatter away out the window all day."

She vanished, and Sara Jane checked the name off her list with the stub of a pencil and moved on down the dirt street.

Watching with keen interest was a man behind a buggy in the street, not 20 feet from Sara Jane as she shouted out the two men's names. Willy Pointer had been walking past, on his way from his boarding house to Main Street and a meeting with Something Smith.

When he heard the woman calling out the names, he ducked behind the rig and listened. The woman's voice meant nothing to him. When she turned and walked directly toward him before she turned up the street, he stiffened.

It was her! The woman asking about him and Something Smith was the woman from the ranch, Mrs. Nelson. What the hell was she doing here in town? Why was she hunting the two of them?

Something Smith would know. He'd have a plan.

Willy hurried down the street and found Something Smith behind the saddle shop, looking in wonder at the new Remington repeater rifle that he held in his hands. He pushed the last cartridge in place and held it out to show to his partner in crime.

"Ain't she a beauty? Got the loan of her from the General Store to see if I want to buy it. I won't."

Willy told him about what he had heard on the street only a few minutes before. Something scowled.

"Damn it to hell! Knew we should have cut down that woman at the ranch. I just had a bad feeling about her and that kill. Damn it!"

Ten minutes later their plan was in place, and Something Smith and Willy Pointer set up their rifles on the roof of the saddle shop across from

the hotel. The place had a false front as most of
the businesses did, pretending to be two-storied.

On the left side of the false front was a hole that
had been left for water to drain off the almost flat
roof. Something Smith rested the rifle barrel on
a pillow he made from his frayed wool jacket. He
lay flat on his belly behind the gun and sighted
on the front door of the Salt River Hotel.

"Like shooting trout in a bucket," he said and
grinned at Pointer.

"Just don't miss, or our asses will be burned
from here to San Francisco."

"I won't miss. What's the range? About thirty-
five yards? How can I miss? What I aim at is what
I hit."

"Yeah, but remember that—"

"Hell, what's to remember? You just make sure
that our horses are behind this place and that the
ladder down from the roof is free and clear. Soon
as I shoot I'll be racing back there, dumping the
rifle and sliding down that ladder like it was a
pole greased with pig fat."

"I'll have it ready. I just wanted to remind you
about the shot. It's more than a little—"

"Shut up, Pointer, and let me concentrate. If I
don't see the bastard come out of the front door,
all bets are canceled."

They both were quiet for a moment, then Something Smith began to hum a catchy little tune as
he stared at the door of the Salt River Hotel.

They waited the rest of the morning.

"Maybe they'll eat dinner at the hotel," Willy
said. He lay on his back on the rough roofing, trying to find a comfortable spot. The sun came down
warm and bright on his belly, and he felt relaxed.

"Maybe they won't come out of the place at
all," Smith said. He wiped his eyes. "I got to keep

sharp. They could come out just any time."

A moment later he tensed. "There. There goes the woman, the one you said had on the yellow dress. Hell, yes, that's Mrs. Nelson all right. Can't forget her tight little ass."

"She came out or went in?"

"Went in, stupid. She was already outside when you saw her. Now if Morgan goes inside, we can nail them both when they come out."

They never saw Buckskin Morgan go into the hotel. They knew there was another entrance, but it opened on the alley and was used mostly for deliveries.

Just past two o'clock Smith yelped as he saw both the woman and Morgan come out the front door of the hotel. They paused a moment, and that's when Smith knew he should have shot but wasn't ready. By the time he sighted in on them again they walked toward him down the three steps.

He sighted again, pulled the trigger and grinned when the Winchester bucked in his hands and the big bullet slammed across the 35 yards toward Buckskin Morgan.

Chapter Nine

Buckskin Morgan and Sara Jane came to the steps and started down the first one when Sara Jane stumbled. Morgan surged forward to catch her just as he heard a rifle fire. The slug tore through the side of his left arm, and he started to fall down the last two steps.

He turned and caught Sara Jane as she flailed her arms trying to keep her balance. They hit the boardwalk hard and rolled once before Buckskin jumped up and sprinted for the far side of the street.

"Somebody shot at us. Run for cover," he shouted at Sara Jane as he started across the street. He had looked up and seen a puff of white smoke coming from the drain hole over the roof of the leather store.

He charged in the front door.

"Where's your back entrance?" he barked.

A surprised saddle maker dropped his mouth

95

open and pointed with his awl to the left and rear. Buckskin raced through a curtain, then over some boxes and stacks of cowhides to the rear door. He fumbled with the latch, and as he did he heard hoofbeats outside.

He got the door open and surged through it, six-gun in hand. He got off one quick shot at the rear end of a black horse vanishing around the end of the alley into the street. Missed.

He ran down the alley and looked for the black horse, but nothing moved on the half a block to Main. Once the bushwhacker got to Main there would be no way to identify him except with a just fired rifle. Impossible. He went on up the side street to Main and back to the hotel.

No sense looking on the roof. The shooter had gone. One man or two? Couldn't tell. The judge or Something Smith? Hard to tell.

He found Sara Jane sitting on a couch in the hotel lobby. She wasn't crying; she was too frightened. She sat there staring at the wall. It took him three tries to get her attention.

When she saw him she leaned into his arms and held him tight.

"I thought you were dead. I thought I was dead. If they had kept on shooting we would have been." She stopped and trembled.

"They're gone, whoever they were. I think you better stay inside the rest of the day. They could try again. Let's go back up to the room. Then I want you to wrap up my arm. It isn't hit bad, but that rifle slug sure ruined a shirt."

Ten minutes later he had his arm bandaged. It was a bleeder, with more blood than damage. They tied it up with strips of cotton cloth torn from one of Sara Jane's petticoats. Her hands still trembled when she tied the knot of the bandage.

"You think they'll try again?"

"No, I think they're scared off for a while. I got a shot at the rear end of one of them, but he was too faraway to tell who he was. Could have been one man or two."

"So what do we do now?"

"I'm going to talk to that newspaper editor again."

"Ginger Hazleton. She's a pretty girl."

"I think she has some idea who the judge might be. It's time I started kicking butt around here and get some answers. I've been the nice guy too long."

Sara Jane smiled. "Just don't start kicking butt with Ginger. You leave that girl alone."

"I promise I won't kick her. Now, you lay down and have a nap. Do you a world of good. I'm off to find the damn judge."

In the judge's office, Percival Laudenhimer sat behind his big desk and scowled at Something Smith and Willy Pointer.

"So it's true. I heard that two assholes tried to gun down Buckskin Morgan on Main Street at high noon. Why the hell you try to do that?"

"Because . . . well, he's been the one asking about you and about me, and I figure he was bad news so I'd just blow him into hell." Something Smith watched the effect of his words on the judge.

"You figured, you thought! Shit! I don't pay you to figure or think. You follow orders. That's what you haven't been doing. I want you to get rid of the man and the woman. I hear she's the widow Nelson you left alive out on her ranch up in the foothills."

Something Smith nodded. "Yeah, figured you wouldn't like that."

"I don't. Now I'm giving you some instructions. Listen closely and follow them to the letter. I want both Morgan and the Nelson woman dead before the sun sets. You get them, but do it neatly and out of town. Anywhere. Get them out of Phoenix into the desert somewhere and kill them. Is that plain enough?"

"Yes, Mr. Laudenhimer."

"Then get out of here. In case you need an idea, why not kidnap the woman to get Morgan out of town and gun them both out there. Now that I've done your thinking for you, go do the job."

Something Smith and Pointer hurried out of the office and down the back stairs to the alley.

"Where do we start?" Pointer asked.

"The hotel."

A few minutes later they ushered the hotel clerk into an empty first floor room, and Pointer held a six-gun muzzle in his gut.

"Ike, you're going to tell us what room that Buckskin Morgan guy rented, or I'm gonna gut shoot you and leave you to die in pain, lots of damn pain. You understand?"

"Registered in room 212."

"They ain't there, dumbass. That's the one that got blown up the other night and they weren't in it. Where are they now?"

The clerk remembered Buckskin's angry instructions and began to sweat.

"They must have moved, but they didn't tell me where they went."

"But they're in this hotel?"

"Yes."

"You know which room. That's your job. Tell me, right now."

"Hell, it isn't worth getting shot for. Room two-sixteen. I checked."

"You sure?"

"Yes."

Something Smith motioned for Pointer to take the gun away. Then before Ike could stop him, Smith caught the man's left arm by the elbow with one hand and the wrist with the other and brought it down sharply on his upthrusting knee.

Ike's arm broke, and a piece of jagged white bone protruded through the flesh. He screamed in pain.

Pointer and Smith left the room and hurried up the stairs as they heard the screams of the room clerk behind them. They rushed to room 216 where Something Smith tried the door handle. It was locked. He stepped back to the wall in the narrow hall, took one step and kicked the sole of his boot hard against the door right beside the knob.

The simple lock jolted open, and the door smashed inward, swinging around until it hit the wall. Sara Jane sat up slowly from where she had been napping on the bed. She stared at the two men who charged into the room. Before she could scream, Smith grabbed her and pressed his hand over her mouth.

"Now, Mrs. Nelson, no reason to get all scared. We're old poking friends of yours, and we've seen you damn near naked. Remember? Hell, we've seen all of your good parts, so just relax. We're going for a little ride in the country. Nice out there this time of day. While we wait out there, we might just have ourselves another little poking party."

Pointer set up the piece of cardboard in the middle of the bed. He smoothed out the quilt, then made sure the message was easy to see. It was exact instructions how to find Sara Jane Nelson again.

Smith picked up Sara Jane and carried her to the door like she was a half-filled sack of potatoes. He looked from the door to the bed and nodded.

"Yeah, that should do it. Now, let's go down the back stairs and get out of here."

An hour later, the two kidnappers and Sara Jane rode up to a small cabin about a mile out of town. It had been a tough trip for them. Sara Jane had screamed until they put a gag around her mouth. They had had trouble carrying her down the back steps.

When two people saw them, they said she was a runaway wife they were taking back home. They didn't trust her on a horse. Smith carried her on his mount just in front of him.

The cabin at the old mine had partly caved in, but the front half was still weatherproof and would stop a few rifle slugs.

They left Sara Jane tied up and checked their firing positions.

"We want a crossfire, so he can't hunker down behind a rock somewhere. He'll know we're in the shack when he gets here. Good part is we can see him coming for a quarter of a mile."

"Except for that little draw down there. It leads up and around this place."

"He won't see that until he gets too committed to use it. We got no problems."

"Where you want me, Something?"

"Take your rifle over behind that mound of slag and fire over that metal ore car. We leave Miss Pussy here in the cabin and take off her gag so she can shout for him. That will help draw him in."

"She'll warn him where we are," Pointer said.

"By that time, he'll be in our sights and have four or five rifle slugs plowing into his body."

"Where do we leave the horses?"

"Tied to the old rail over there, right out in the open, so he'll know for damn sure we're here."

Pointer took the horses over and tied them, came back and looked down the open vista toward Phoenix. All he saw was one lonesome hawk with its jagged wings circling in endless rising columns of heated air.

Inside, Something Smith stood in front of Sara Jane where he had pushed her down on a bench. He took the gag from her mouth and watched her spit and try to recover from a dry mouth.

"You're a stinking animal!" she shouted.

"Right, and I'm feeling like it's breeding time again. Let's you and me do some fancy fucking."

Pointer shook his head. "Not me, Something. Last time she grazed one of my balls when she was kicking."

"All mine," Smith said. He left her hands and feet tied for the time, pulled her blouse up to her neck and put both hands on her breasts.

"Damn, she's got fair tits, know that?"

"If'n you get it into her, you do it alone," Pointer said. "I ain't in no mood to help you rape her again."

"Well, well, well. Look who's getting religion at this late date. Go on, get out of here. I'll handle her."

Sara Jane scowled at the big man. She almost had her hands untied in back of her, and she'd felt a piece of wood, sharp on one end and not much bigger than a lead pencil. If only she had time.

Pointer left the shack, then came right back in. "Might be we've got company. I saw a dust trail about a half mile out there. Looked like a rider moving fast."

"Damn," Smith said. "You stay here with your rifle. I changed my mind. I'll go over by that old mine shaft and the ore car, and we'll both nail him soon as he gets off his horse."

Pointer looked at Sara Jane.

"You knucklehead, Pointer. She's tied up. She can't hurt you none."

Something Smith ran low across the open space to the ore car and hid. Pointer took one look at Sara Jane, checked the bindings on her feet, then hurried to the window that had no glass in it.

"Somebody coming for damn sure," he said. The trail of dust rising from the horse's four shod hooves had been there just a moment before, but now the dust had vanished.

Behind him, Sara Jane fumbled with the cords. She nearly had them undone. Just a few more minutes.

"Damn, he's gone. Where could a man and a horse go? Christ, he's into that gully. He could come up anywhere along there. He could make us sitting ducks out here on this flat."

"So get on your horse and ride out before he kills you," Sara Jane said. "You know that's what he's going to do. He'll kill you sure as God is in his heaven."

"Shut up, woman. I got me enough troubles out here."

Sara Jane had one hand free. She pulled and twisted the cords to get enough slack to slip her other hand free.

She watched him now, praying that he wouldn't check her hands. When he turned and looked at her, she kept her arms absolutely still.

"You're afraid of me, aren't you, Pointer?" she asked.

"You kill Larson back there in San Carlos Wells?"

"Might have. If I did he deserved it. Do you deserve it for what you did to my husband?"

"Shut up, woman. I got to watch out here."

She slid her left hand out of the cord and rubbed her wrists. Her fingers searched until she found the splinter of wood she had found. It was six inches long she figured, one end needle-sharp, the other end chopped flat.

How would she hold it? Like a dagger? No, too hard to hit a target that way. Like a lance. She worked the stick between her third and fourth finger with the sharp point outward. Slowly she adjusted it until the flat part nestled in her palm.

If she kept the sliver straight out from her fist in line with her forearm, she'd have a powerful weapon.

"Damn, I think he's coming!" Pointer whispered. "I can see him moving cautious-like up toward us from the edge of the gully way out there. Not much cover there. I track him just right and then catch him on his next move and I can blast him into hell. Yes, yes, come on, move, Buckskin Morgan. Move your ass right into my sights and you're one dead cowboy."

Sara Jane reached down and worked on the cord holding her ankles together. A moment later she had the knot untied and was free. She picked up the wooden dagger, put it between her fingers as before and stood without a sound. She took one step forward.

"Yes, move, Buckskin Morgan, you bastard. Move just once more."

Sara Jane lunged forward, holding the heavy splinter straight out and aimed at Pointer's exposed back as he sighted down his rifle.

She saw him hear her coming, but he stayed with his shot. Just before he pulled the trigger, she reached him and the sharp point of the splinter drove into his side, slashing through two inches of his flesh, slanting off a rib and leaving a two-inch bloody gash.

Pointer bellowed in agony, turned, dropped the rifle and faced her. Sara Jane acted on impulse, on the age-old instinct to save her own life.

She held the bloody splinter in front of her and lunged again, aiming at his chest. He tried to dodge, but he slammed into the old table. Before he could recover and jolt the other way, the wooden dagger sliced into his chest, detoured half an inch around a rib and plunged through his heart.

Sara Jane screamed in fear mixed with anger, let go of the wooden splinter and cowered away from the mortally wounded man. His eyes looked at her for a moment, then rolled up in their sockets. His knees gave way, and then his whole body collapsed and crumpled to the floor, dead long before he sprawled on the rotting wooden planks.

Outside she heard two rifle shots, neither of which hit the shack. She stepped around the bloody body on the floor and peeked out the broken window. She saw Something Smith firing off to the left. A figure there moved, hunkered down behind a rock pile, then darted forward, diving behind rocks taken from the old mine.

Pointer's rifle! She picked it up, worked the lever at the bottom and saw a new round slide into the breech. She lifted it to shoot at Something Smith, but he was gone. Too late she saw him running across the open space between her and the horses.

Furiously she swung the rifle, trying to aim at him. She couldn't keep up. Then he was almost at the horse. When she pulled the trigger the recoil drove her back away from the window. She looked through the window again. Something Smith had mounted and rode straight away from the cabin to the right, making himself the smallest target he possibly could for the rifleman far behind him.

Chapter Ten

Something Smith rode hard and fast away from the cabin. The rifleman behind him had a small, diminishing target, and six shots failed to stop the fleeing man.

Sara Jane watched out the window a moment, then she looked at the blood on her hands and stared a moment at the sprawled body on the floor. She screeched in terror and ran out the sagging door.

The bright sunshine stunned her for a moment, and she stopped, looked around in wonder and turned as she heard someone running toward her. Automatically she held out her hands to protect herself.

"No, no, go away. Leave me alone." The words came out stilted, without anger or force.

"Sara Jane, it's all right. He's gone. I'm Buckskin Morgan. I'm your friend. Don't be afraid. It's me, Buckskin."

She frowned and stared at him, and a moment later recognition broke over her features as she ran two steps to him and fell into his arms.

She shuddered and took two deep breaths.

"I killed him. I killed the other one inside the shack."

Buckskin held her away from him. She nodded. "He was going to shoot you, and I got untied and stabbed him." Her whisper turned into a shriek. "He's dead. Oh, Lord, but it hurts deep down like it's burning on my soul. Blood all over my hand."

She held out her right hand, and he saw that blood had splattered her fingers.

Buckskin held her, and they walked over to the remains of the cabin. He started through the door, but she pushed away from him.

"I don't want to see it again."

Buckskin nodded and stepped inside. The man lay on his back, one arm under him, legs flailed out, the shirt at his left side bloody and matted against him. A jagged splinter of wood extended out of his chest three inches.

That was about where his heart would be. No man could live through that. He bent and checked for any pulse at his throat. Nothing. A fired rifle cartridge lay on the littered floor. He saw discarded strips of folded rags that could have been used to tie up or gag a person. He tried to imagine what had happened inside.

The two bushwhackers had split up for a crossfire, one at the pile of rocks by the ore car, the other one here. Evidently Sara Jane had slipped out of her bindings, wounded him in the side, then stabbed him in the heart. Amazing.

Buckskin hurried outside. Sara Jane stood where he had left her.

"I killed him," she said, her voice back to a dull flatness that worried Buckskin.

"He's the man who raped you, who killed your husband. I would have killed him if I'd had the chance."

"I killed him." Sara Jane wasn't looking at Buckskin. She stared into the distance.

Buckskin caught her hand and talked gently to her.

"Sara Jane, we're going to go back to town. There's a horse over here, and I'll help you get up on him. Then we'll walk to where I left my horse, all right?"

Sara Jane didn't respond. She held his hand tightly. When he stepped ahead, she walked beside him.

It took them ten minutes to both get mounted, then they rode slowly back toward town. Sara Jane volunteered nothing. She responded softly and with few words when she spoke. That worried Buckskin. She hadn't reacted this hard when she killed Larson. Buckskin knew he had to be careful how he handled her.

It was nearly sunset by the time they stopped in front of the Salt River Hotel. Buckskin paid a young boy a quarter to lead the two horses back to the livery and turn them in.

Upstairs, Buckskin checked out another empty room, 224, and moved their gear into it. He let Sara Jane sit down on the bed, then he locked the door and put a chair under it.

She looked up and blinked. "I'm feeling better, Buckskin. I really am. I've never felt that way before. It was such a dark mood, so dreadful, and I felt like I was the one who should die. I've never felt that way. I got free from my bindings and I found that sharp stick and . . ."

She looked away.

"You don't have to talk about it. You don't even have to think about it now. It's done. You rest up and you'll feel better. They would have killed us both if they could have. You know that. Something is going on here we don't know about. Now it's my job to find out what it is."

She frowned. "You be careful. I . . . I don't want to have your death on my conscience."

Buckskin grinned and kissed her forehead. "Hey, exactly my feelings on the subject. I've got a lot of things to do yet."

He watched her. Her color was back, the paleness gone. She looked at him, and he caught a small flash in her green eyes.

"Can I bring you something to eat from the dining room?"

She shook her head. "Not up to food yet. Maybe tomorrow."

"I need to go see what I can dig up on the street. Somebody's got to know who the judge is. He's got to be the one behind all of this."

She frowned, her eyes clouded. "Be careful."

"Always." He pulled out his Colt and checked the five rounds, spun the cylinder, then made sure it was on the empty tube and let down the hammer gently. "I'll be back."

Five minutes later, he walked out of the first saloon. No sign of Something Smith. The man was running scared, but he would still use the saloons. Which one?

He had just left the second saloon, when he sensed someone behind him. He spun around and saw a man ten feet away with a six-gun already in his hand.

Buckskin stabbed at his right hip for this Colt. His hand jolted the butt of the weapon upward.

In the same motion his palm closed around the butt and his finger slid into the trigger guard. The upward motion lifted the revolver from leather. The fraction of a second the muzzle cleared the holster, Buckskin rammed it forward in a point and shoot move.

As he pointed, he dove to his belly on the boardwalk, cushioning his dive with his left hand and triggering the Colt with his right first finger.

Both revolvers went off at nearly the same time. The assailant didn't have time to adjust his aim as his target moved. His round went three feet over Buckskin's head. Buckskin's round drilled straight and true into the man's chest.

The man in the town suit jolted backwards. The revolver flew out of his hand, and his face went wild for a moment with panic. Then he was out of Buckskin's view as he slammed into the board-walk on his back.

Buckskin came to his knees, thumbing back the Colt's hammer and bringing a new .45 round into the firing chamber. He got one foot under him and surged to his feet, the Colt still covering the man lying on the boardwalk.

It wasn't dark yet, but dusk was coming quickly. The man on the boards hadn't moved. Buck-skin walked up quickly and kicked the revolver out of reach and squatted beside him. A small bloodstain and a burned hole through a blue shirt showed where Buckskin's round had hit him.

A short, balding man knelt beside the body.

"Who are you?" the short man asked.

"Buckskin Morgan. Who are you?"

"I'm a doctor." The medic touched the man's throat, then his forehead and pinched his nose.

He sighed. "Well, this one is dead. Somebody go get the sheriff." He looked up at Buckskin. "You kill him?"

"Afraid so. He drew down on me about to shoot me in the back. Must have been half a dozen people saw him."

"I saw it," a man from the growing crowd said. "He was gonna shoot this man like he said. Damn miracle that he didn't."

"Well, I guess that gets you free and clear," the medic said. "Sheriff should be here soon. I saw it all happen, too." He frowned. "How could you shoot so straight, diving to the ground that way?"

"Lucky shot, I guess. You know this man?" Buckskin asked.

The doctor looked around. "Seen him. Last I knew he worked for a merchant named Laudenhimer. Don't know if he does now." He had spoken in a whisper. "If it comes up, you didn't hear this from me. I don't want to get involved."

A short time later, Sheriff Abady arrived. He scowled at Buckskin, took his verbal statement, then asked four of the bystanders including the doctor what they had witnessed. At last he was satisfied.

"I'll write out a statement, and I want you to come down to the office and sign it."

"Is that necessary?"

"It is. I like to keep everything neat and my own behind covered in case I get any trouble from some citizen."

Buckskin went down to the small sheriff's office and signed the paper, then headed back to the hotel. He'd had enough action for one day. He figured the best thing he could do was be a friend for Sara Jane.

A half hour later, down the dark street from the Salt River Hotel, Percival Laudenhimer sat in his office and scowled at the man across from him.

"Sheriff Abady, you let him sign a statement of self-defense and let him get away? The dead man was one of my investigators. You knew that. He did a lot of work for me."

"Including shooting men on the street in broad daylight?"

"None of your damn business. Did you bring the papers?"

"I did. I still don't like it. If you say you can make it stand up, I'll go along with you." Sheriff Abady scowled. "This better be damn important. I could get ten years in the territorial prison for doing this."

"No risk, no gain, Sheriff. It's like I told you before."

"My re-election campaign?" the sheriff said.

"As soon as we get it done, I'll give you a bank draft."

"No. Absolutely not. Nothing on paper. I want double eagles, as we agreed—a thousand dollars worth."

"You'll get it. Now, do we really have to go to the steps of the county courthouse to do this?"

"That's what the law says—an open auction. It doesn't say anything about how loud I have to talk, or what time it has to be held. Let's go."

The sheriff and Percival Laudenhimer left the merchant's second floor office, went out the front door and down a block to the county courthouse. It was only a small wooden building half a block over from Main. The vacant area in front covered half a city block and would be the site of the new stone courthouse when the county found money enough to start building it.

Now various county functions were carried out in different buildings around town. The pair stopped on the steps and looked around. Nobody was within hearing distance. Even so, the sheriff kept his voice to a stage whisper.

"Be it known to all here assembled, that I, as sheriff of the county of Maricopa in the Territory of Arizona, do now offer the following property for sale in lieu of back taxes. The property is known as the Nelson ranch, legal description entailed. Due and owing on the property is the sum of three hundred and sixty-eight dollars. The bidding is now open for this property with a minimum bid of the stated amount."

Laudenhimer grinned. "I bid the stated amount."

Sheriff Abady looked around and waited a moment. "Since I hear no other bids for this property, I hereby declare it sold at a legal sheriff's auction in and for the county of Maricopa, Territory of Arizona, on this day, August 14, 1882."

"Well, Sheriff, I guess that does it. Let's go back to my office for a toast. I have some fine whiskey in my bottom drawer for occasions like this."

"And that bag of double eagles you promised me," the sheriff said.

"Of course. I always keep my promises. Right this way. To a new rich man, you, and a soon to be extremely rich man—me."

Back in the Salt River Hotel, Buckskin Morgan carried a tray from the dining room. It was covered with a linen napkin, and under it were two dinners of turkey, stuffing, mashed potatoes, gravy and cranberry sauce.

He let himself in the locked door and saw Sara Jane sit up quickly on the bed. She rubbed one eye and took a deep breath.

"Oh, I must have dozed off. I had the most wonderful dream." She stopped and shook her head. "But I still remember what happened out there today."

"You should remember. That's not the sort of thing you forget. You simply did what you had to to survive. Nothing wrong with that. The simple fact is that you probably saved not only your own life but mine as well, and I'm forever grateful."

He grinned and set the tray on the bed beside her.

"So grateful that I brought you a late supper. Don't tell me you're not hungry. I had to bribe the cook and the dining room manager to get this tray made up as it is."

He took off the napkin, and Sara Jane's eyes lit up.

"Oh, turkey, my favorite. It reminds me of the big family Thanksgiving dinners we used to have on the farm."

They hesitated a moment, then both grabbed forks and began to eat.

A half hour later, the supper was over, the coffee gone as well as most of the food. Sara Jane grinned.

"Looks like I was hungrier than I thought. Now, I'd like to be alone for a while. Oh, you can come back and sleep here, but I need an hour or so to think through the rest of this. I just might not want to see any more of Something Smith. I even shot at him today with the rifle, but I didn't even come close."

Buckskin picked up the tray with the dishes and nodded.

"Understand. I'll take these back to the kitchen and see if I can find Smith in the saloons. He must be out there somewhere trying to drink himself senseless. Seems like what he'd do."

Buckskin bent and kissed her forehead. She looked up with a smile of thanks as he left the room, locking it from the outside behind him.

Ten minutes later, he wandered past the newspaper office. He wanted to check with Ginger Hazleton about a merchant named Laudenhimer. She would know about him if anyone in town did. He saw a light on in the front office and rapped on the door. A minute later Ginger came toward him and he waved at her.

She unlocked the door, let him in and locked it again.

"Well, Mr. Morgan, what are you doing out at this time of night?"

"And what are you doing still working at this hour of the night?"

"Working," she said and smiled.

"Me, too. I want to ask you about a man I heard about today. You have a minute?"

"How about some coffee and a piece of cherry pie?"

"Sounds delightful. I could eat half your pie."

She smiled and led him up the stairs to her quarters. A lamp burned in the living room. They went into the kitchen, and she took out a freshly baked pie.

"I was hoping you would come again," she said.

"I was hoping that you would be working late."

They stood in the kitchen close together. Buckskin bent slightly and moved toward her lips. She waited for him, then at the last moment she whimpered and lifted to meet his kiss. His arms went around her, and she sighed even before the embrace was over.

When the kiss ended, Ginger caught his hand and walked across the kitchen toward her bedroom.

"Buckskin Morgan, ever since I first met you, I've been running a fever wanting to see you naked." She picked up the lamp in the living room. "This looks like a fine time for us to get a whole lot better acquainted."

Ginger pushed open the door to her bedroom, put the lamp on the dresser and sat down on the bed. She patted the spot beside her.

"Come here, Lee Buckskin Morgan. I want to see if you are as delicious as you look."

Chapter Eleven

When Buckskin sat on the bed beside Ginger, she turned and kissed him hard on the lips, then spun away from him, standing in front and watching him, her blue eyes gleaming.

"Morgan, don't get in a rush. When I get feeling this way, all hot and sexy and wanting just to hump you like wild, I get a little crazy and do strange things. Right now I'm so hot I think I'm already wet and dripping down below, but for that you'll have to wait."

She did a little dance in front of him, swinging her hips and shaking her breasts, then suddenly she sat on his lap, straddling him and pushing her legs past him on the bed. She kissed him half a dozen times, then caught one of his hands and put it over her right breast.

"My titties want to say hello. Squeeze them a little, but just don't get rough. I don't allow any

117

rough play. Gentle and soft will get my clothes off . . . eventually."

She unbuttoned his shirt and spread it apart, then played with the black hair on his chest.

"Oh, yes! I like chest hair. Makes a man different from a woman." She giggled. "Lots of interesting ways a man is different, and I'm real glad of that."

She pulled his shirt out of his pants and took it off his shoulders. Then she leaned in so she could nibble at his hard nipples.

"Strange how a man's breasts just never grow. Glad mine did though." She stood in front of him and slowly began to unbutton the top of her dress. "I bet you like tits. Look like the kind of a man who would go for titties more than legs. Yes, you're a tit man. I can see it in your face."

She opened the last button at her waist, then lifted her camisole to show her breasts. They were large and perfectly formed with large areolas.

"Like my girls? You can touch them if you want to, but be gentle."

Each of Buckskin's hands found a breast, and he caressed them with a feather touch, then tweaked her nipples. She had thrown her head back, and her breath came fast and hard now. A soft moan came from her throat, and he could see her hips doing a little dance all their own.

He bent forward and kissed one of her breasts.

Ginger gasped, then smiled down at him and nodded. "Oh, yes, the girls really like to be kissed and sucked and nibbled on. You be nice to them, and they'll be nice to you."

He worked around one breast and bit gently on her nipple, which had doubled in size and now pulsated hard. He licked it and then sucked as much of her breast into his mouth as he could.

Ginger gave a little cry of wonder, pulled away from him and collapsed on the bed beside him. She pulled her dress open, moved the camisole up and smiled at him.

"Go right on with what you were doing, lover. I couldn't stand up anymore."

He finished the other breast, and she moaned and sighed and pulled him down on the bed and rolled over on top of him.

"Buckskin, big whanger, why do you like to fuck?" She giggled. "Fuck, fuck, fuck, fucker. There I said it. Now tell me, Buckskin Morgan, why do you like to fuck?"

"Same reason you do. At the moment it seems like exactly the right thing to do. Most women take more working up and convincing than men do. I've never met a woman yet who didn't like to fuck up a bloody storm, once she finally gets in a real sexy mood."

"Sometimes it doesn't take much convincing for me," Ginger said and grinned. "I know that sounds wicked, but why should it be wrong for a woman to have a sexy good time like this when it isn't wrong for the man?"

"I don't think it is wrong. The only problem is the woman must be careful not to get pregnant. That's the big social drawback for a woman."

She nodded, then pulled his mouth back to her breast. "I wonder if humans were ever like cattle? You know, when one bull had thirty or forty cows and heifers to breed. Hey, how would you like to have a harem of thirty sexy females and your only job was to get each one pregnant every year?"

Buckskin laughed. "I'd be worn down to a nub and too tired to enjoy life."

"You mean you don't enjoy poking a woman?"

"Absolutely, and the prettier and sexier the better. But thirty? I don't think I'd make a good range bull. I'd rather concentrate on one at a time, try to give her all the pleasure I could as we make gentle love in her bedroom."

"Like now?"

"Like now. Let's get you out of that dress."

Ginger grinned, sat up, flipped the skirt out from under her and lifted the dress off over her head. She took the camisole with it, and Buckskin grinned when he saw her big breasts swinging free. They had wide pink areolas and dark red flushed nipples as thick as his thumb.

"Beautiful," he said softly, then he bent and kissed them again. She held his head tightly to her breasts.

"I love that. With you eating away on my titties I'm almost in heaven. Just one place I'd rather you ate your fill of."

She pushed him back and worked at his belt. She opened it and then undid the buttons down his fly. She pushed his pants apart, found his short cotton underwear and worked through them.

Ginger squealed in delight when she found his hard prick. She worked it out of his underwear and whimpered as she bent to kiss the purple head.

"Marvelous!" she cried. "So wonderful. To think he could grow from a little worm into such a big whanger. Oh, damn, I want you naked right now."

She stood and pulled off his boots, then his pants and slowly, carefully took down his short underwear to let his erection jolt out.

Ginger yelped in wonder. "My God, but he's big. I don't know if there's room in . . ." She chuckled. Buckskin kicked off the underwear and reached for her half-petticoats and slid them down. Then she lay on the bed clad only in her soft, silk bloomers. He reached for them, but she caught his hands.

"Not quite yet." She got on her knees on the bed and bent a little so she could feed one breast after the other into his mouth. He chewed and kissed and licked them until she was puffing like a steam engine.

She dropped on the bed and pulled her bloomers off in one quick move, then pushed him down and rolled on top of him, pressing hard with her hips on his erection.

"I've always wanted to do this," she whispered. "Lie on top this way."

He brought his hands up her legs, worked into her inner thighs and caressed her gently. She made room for his hands by lifting her hips a little until his fingers found her heartland and massaged her moist place. Finding her hard little node, he twanged it half a dozen times.

Ginger's eyes went wide. Her mouth started to form some words, but before she could she jolted into a wild climax, shaking and quivering and then gasping as the spasms shook her and rocked her back and forth like a rowboat caught in a high wave.

At last she let out a long breath and collapsed on top of him, panting to get her breath back.

When she could talk she looked down at him in delighted surprise.

"What in the world was that all about? That's never happened before."

"You didn't know about your clit, that little hard place down there?"

"I knew something was there, just never touched it before. No one ever has."

"You've never climaxed like that?"

She shook her head. "I've only been naked with a man like this twice. Neither time it went well. The first was when we both were just sixteen and neither of us knew what we were doing. He got excited and spurted all over me, and then he got scared and ran out of the house.

"The other time was on a picnic in the woods back home. The boy got inside of me, but it hurt and he shot it into me almost at once. Then he rolled over and ran into the water for a swim. I . . . I didn't know what to do."

"Boys have to learn about girls, too," Buckskin said.

"But you know about us, I bet. You know what makes us feel best and where to touch." She paused, and her pretty face took on a frown. "Is it better with you deep inside me?"

"We'll find out."

"Right now," she said. "Poke me right now, Morgan!"

He grinned, pushed her on her back, spread her legs and then found her softness again with his fingers. He massaged her moist outer lips and then felt her juices start to flow. He pushed one finger deep inside her, and she purred softly.

He entered her slowly and gently, letting her juices lubricate both of them, and a moment later he was fully in. Tears glistened in her eyes.

"That was so wonderful, so beautiful. I can't describe how marvelous that feels. Not at all like the other time."

"It gets better," he said. Buckskin was starting to feel his own pressure. He stroked once gently, then again, and the third time he felt her hips rise to his.

"Oh, glory," she said. "Oh, glory, glory, glory!"

He pounded harder and hit her clit six times. Her eyes went wide, and a moment later both of them ripped into climaxes that made them slam together a dozen times. He exploded inside her, and she disintegrated in three hard climaxes of her own, trembling and gasping when they shook her so hard.

She opened her eyes and stared up at him. He smiled and kissed her, then eased down on her. They both relaxed and gasped in enough air to come fully alive again.

Neither of them talked for five minutes, then he eased away from her and lay beside her on the bed, holding her hand, his arm under her shoulders.

Ginger looked at him, tears in her eyes. "I don't think it could ever be any better than that was," she said. "I want to be with you forever, no matter who you are or where you go or what you do. I'm yours forevermore."

He smiled and held her tightly.

Later she sat up and stared down at him. "Men are so different. Muscles all over the place, a hard little belly and tough stomach and no breasts at all. Your hips are narrow. I guess because you don't have to bear children. I've never really had the chance to look at a man all naked before. I like it."

Buckskin sat up and chuckled. "Glad you like it, otherwise you'd be in for a tough life. Being a woman is an important thing, and it's best if she enjoys being with men—at least with her husband when she gets one."

She sat up beside him and kissed his cheek.

"I'm still trying to find out who the judge is," he said. "You do any more thinking on it?"

"A bit. I have an idea who he could be. Not sure, mind you, but an idea. One man in town owns five of the businesses that I know of, and I'd guess he's a silent partner in half a dozen more. He wants to run the town and the whole territory. His name is Percival Laudenhimer."

"Good news. That's a lot more than I have to go on. This Laudenhimer, is he a model citizen or a bully and a legal crook?"

"Oh, he's a legal crook. He's foreclosed on two business firms I know of. The county clerk is a good friend of mine and tells me little things now and then."

"Like what?"

"Oh, county business that's coming up. Today he told me that he'd written formal legal orders confiscating the property of three people who hadn't paid taxes for three years. That's the legal limit, he told me. The land goes into a holding pattern until the sheriff holds a sheriff's auction of the property on the courthouse steps."

She frowned a minute. "Say, one of the names seemed familiar. I've got the list downstairs. It's something we always print, so maybe some of the family will come forward and pay the taxes before they lose their property. Let's slip down there and get the paper off my desk."

"Naked?" Buckskin asked.

"Why not? It's my building. I can run all over it naked if I want to." She laughed, stood up and walked to the stairway.

Ginger laughed softly as she stepped through to the front, scurried to her desk, fumbled a moment and then came back with the slip of paper.

"Got it," she said. They went to the lamp burning on the old press, and she looked at the names. "What was the name of the dead man again?"

"James Nelson," Buckskin said.

"Oh, that's what I thought. Here it is. His place has been put on the takeover list. He owes three hundred and sixty-eight dollars in back taxes."

"When will it be auctioned off?"

"Could be anytime. I heard about it this afternoon. Someone always tells me when something important is happening."

"Sara Jane didn't say anything about back taxes. Doesn't seem to me like the sort of thing a rancher would slip up on. I'll have to ask her about that."

They went back upstairs and sat on the edge of the bed.

She grinned at him. "I like being this way, sitting here naked with you, and you all bare, too. Never done anything like this before. I really like it."

"Don't get to like it too much. This sort of thing is usually for married ladies, you know."

"I heard that. I just didn't know it was so much fun, so exciting, so button-busting wonderful."

When he kissed her cheek she tried to pull him down on the bed, but he held her up.

"You're mean. But then I don't know if I could stand any more wonderful sex tonight or not. Oh, yes!" She jumped up and her breasts shook and jolted and bounced, and Buckskin grinned just watching them.

"Hey, now, pay attention. I just thought of something strange. There's an old prospector in town. He's been around here long as there's been a town, they say. Usually he's unshaven, dirty, sunburned to a turn, his clothes ragged and patched and torn again. Sometimes I let him sleep on a cot in back when he's in town and out of money.

"Today I saw him. It took me three turns to recognize him. His name is Try Again something or other. He was shaved, he was clean, his hair was cut and combed, and he had on brand-new clothes, not fancy, but new and clean. He even had on town shoes.

"Now to a suspicious person like me, a newspaper woman, that means there has to be a story there. Either he quit prospecting and found himself a woman who made him clean himself up before she would let him bed her, or old Try Again found himself a rich strike somewhere."

"Getting interesting," Buckskin said. "Where is most of the mining around here?"

"Up on the Mogollon Rim, thirty to forty miles northeast of us."

"That doesn't help me much. The Nelson place is almost due east of here."

"Not any mines in that area that I know of," Ginger said.

"Afraid of that. Try Again might not be much help to us. How does a piece of property get put up for the sheriff's sale in this territory?"

"Same as most, I'd reckon. If the taxes aren't paid for three years running, it's advertised for two months, the property owners are contacted by registered mail, then the deadline passes and the auction can take place."

"What if the taxes were paid? How could the same piece of land be auctioned?"

"You mean somebody trying to get the land so they kill the owner, scare the widow and change the records so they could put the land up for sale?"

"About what I was wondering," Buckskin said.

"It would be tough, but possible. The county clerk and the tax collector would have to be in on it, or it would have to be done late at night. Payment records would have to be wiped out, if the taxes were paid."

"Tomorrow let's go have a look at those county records and a friendly chat with the county clerk and tax gatherer."

A sudden noise came from downstairs. They looked at each other as the same pounding sounded again, as if someone knocked continually on the front door. Buckskin dressed and waved at Ginger. "I'll go down and see who it is. Must be something important."

Two minutes later, Buckskin pushed the shirt in his pants and fastened his belt. He carried the lighted lamp in one hand and opened the front door with the other. A man stood there about ready to hit the door again with a rock.

"Let me in. I got nowhere else to go."

"Who are you?" Buckskin asked.

The man looked up and shook his head. "Damned if I remember. Had me a drink or two."

Buckskin heard Ginger come up behind him. She looked past him and gasped.

"Try Again, what happened to you? You were so elegant this afternoon. Now you look like you were dragged behind a stagecoach from here to El Paso."

"Don't know what happened. Had me a dollar and it paid for a few drinks, then they threw me out into the street."

Ginger ducked under Buckskin's arm, caught hold of the old prospector in his new but now filthy and torn clothes and helped him inside.

"You come in. I have your usual cot back where you can sleep it off. Tomorrow I'll make

you a pot of coffee and a big breakfast and
you can tell me what happened to you today.
It must have been a terrific reversal of fortunes
for you."

Chapter Twelve

Buckskin Morgan left Ginger tucking in the old prospector. He went back to the hotel by the side streets and an alley and let himself into their new room as quietly as possible. He hoped that no one had seen him or followed him. He paused just inside the darkened room and waited. No one tried to break down the door.

He looked over at the bed and in a swatch of moonlight coming through the window saw that Sara Jane slept peacefully. He hoped it wouldn't take her long to bounce back from the terror that had consumed her when she killed the man. In a few days she should be back to normal.

He undressed and eased into bed beside her. She awakened for a moment, smiled, reached out and touched him, then slipped back to her own dreams almost at once.

Buckskin grinned as he thought about the developments of the day. One more of the killers had met his maker. Two down and one to go. Most important, they now had a suspect for the judge they had been looking for. That and the listing of the Nelson's ranch for a sheriff's sale were both big developments he'd check out in the morning.

Just after eight the next morning, Buckskin walked into the county clerk's office. He had taken Sara Jane to breakfast in the hotel dining room, then left her barricaded in their room with a chair under the door. She had felt better but wanted to stay in the room during the day.

He didn't tell her about the new clues, but he did ask her if her husband had paid the county taxes on the ranch.

"Of course. James and I talked about everything like that. He made sure that the taxes were paid before we bought our groceries or supplies for the ranch. Twice a year he paid the county taxes to be sure we wouldn't lose the place."

It was as Buckskin had expected, and he figured it was the best clue he'd had so far in this developing mystery. Somebody wanted the Nelsons off their place. The questions were who and why.

A secretary said the county clerk wasn't in yet, so Buckskin waited. He sat on a pine bench and tried to think through the whole mystery of the killed rancher, but nothing much new came to mind.

Ten minutes later, a small man with wire-rimmed spectacles, a trim black business suit and a pipe dangling from his mouth came bustling into the office. He took off his black hat and placed it carefully on a cabinet near his desk and sat in a chair behind the work space. The secretary talked to the small man a moment, then the county clerk came forward.

"Mr. Morgan, you wanted to see the county clerk? That's me, Maynard Rogers. What can I do for you?"

"I'm interested in the ownership history of the James Nelson ranch about fifteen miles east of San Carlos Wells. Are you familiar with the parcel?"

"Yes, unfortunately. The owners fell behind in their taxes and did not respond to notification. The property was put on the sheriff's sale list yesterday, as I recall."

"That's interesting, Mr. Rogers. The widow Nelson claims she has legal receipts for the payment of those taxes. How do you prove someone hasn't paid taxes?"

"If it isn't recorded in our books, then the taxes haven't been paid. It's quite simple. Happens all the time. We have three parcels for the next sheriff's sale."

"When will that be?"

"Whenever the sheriff decides to hold the sale. You'll have to contact his office about that."

Buckskin drummed his fingers on the countertop where the two of them stood. "Mr. Rogers, I'm not accusing you of anything, but is there any way that the record of payments for those past three years on the Nelson ranch could be erased or deleted somehow from the records?"

The county clerk scowled. "I take that to be a personal insult, sir. Nobody handles those account books but me and my assistant. The very thought is preposterous. I'll thank you to apologize."

"I did before I asked the question. Seems to me you and your assistant should take a rather close look at the records on that ranch. The taxes were paid, all legal and proper. Now someone says they weren't, and the ranch is up for sale. Someone is going to get in a lot of trouble. Take a look at your records, Mr. Rogers. I'll be back to talk with you about it tomorrow."

Roger's face turned pale as Buckskin left the office without a backward glance.

Buckskin left the small courthouse and hurried up the street to the newspaper office. He wondered how Ginger Hazleton had fared with her favorite drunk, Try Again.

He opened the office door and walked in. No one was in the front, so he went toward the back.

"I don't want to drink no more damned coffee. My back teeth are floating now."

Buckskin recognized the old prospector's voice. He walked beyond the press and saw Try Again sitting up on the cot and holding his head. Ginger stood in front of him with a coffeepot in one hand and a big cup in the other.

"Try Again, you need more coffee. I want to get you cold stone sober, then you can tell me what happened. It might make a good story for the front page this week."

"Ain't no damn story," Try Again wheezed, then he slid down on the cot. By the time Buckskin walked over to the pair, the old drunk prospector was snoring the sleep of the sotted.

Ginger looked at Buckskin and shook her head. "I've tried everything I know. I just can't get him sobered up. He did wash his hands and face, but he almost threw up when I offered him breakfast."

Buckskin chuckled. "A man on a real drunk can't tolerate food, Ginger. He must have had over half a bottle of whiskey last night. That's enough to keep him drunk for the rest of the day. You won't get anything out of him about what happened to him until late tonight, maybe tomorrow."

They left Try Again where he lay and went out to the front office. Ginger sat in her editor's chair, and Buckskin perched on her paper strewn desk. He told her about his talk with the county clerk.

She scowled for a moment, then rubbed the wrinkles out of her forehead. "If the records were changed to show no payment, I'm sure that Maynard Rogers had nothing to do with it. He certainly can find out if there were any payments blotted out or erased or removed somehow. Let's give him half a day to worry about it. He'll discover the problem if it's there.

"I'd say our next step is to go see the sheriff and tell him there's been a mistake and that he shouldn't offer the Nelson ranch in his next auction."

"If this is an illegal way to get the Nelson ranch, five will get you fifty that the sale has already been held."

"This morning?" Ginger asked.

"Is there any set time for these auctions to be held—by law, I mean?"

"None I've ever heard of. Usually they take place at noon on the courthouse steps." Ginger frowned. "Let's go have a talk with Sheriff Abady," Ginger said. "I never have liked that man."

"What about the tax collector's records?" Buckskin asked. "If it was a conspiracy of some kind to cover up the payments, wouldn't the tax collector have to be in on it as well?"

Ginger nodded. "I was thinking the same thing. He's the next man we visit after we have our little chat with the sheriff."

A short time later in the sheriff's office, Ginger asked a question that riled the lawman.

"What in blazes do you mean by fast, Miss Hazleton? I held the auction when I thought it should be held. There weren't no bidders on two of the properties, and I'll hold a second auction as the law says."

"Which property sold, Sheriff Abady?" Buckskin asked.

"It's on public record at the courthouse, if you want to know, but since I figure you'll go look, I'll tell you. The James Nelson ranch out east of San Carlos Wells sold."

"Who bought it?" Buckskin asked, anger showing in his voice.

Sheriff Abady scowled and took a step back from his desk. "Well, now, I'm through being civil to you. You want to know you go ask the county clerk. The papers should be filed in a day or two, changing the ownership of the property. I don't have to tell you one damned thing more."

"What you forgot to say, Sheriff Abady, is that you're busy and would appreciate our leaving, isn't that right?" Ginger said, staring hard at the lawman. He didn't answer. They went to the door of the small office.

"Election coming up in nine months, Sheriff," Ginger said. "I wonder if you've filed for election yet?"

"Can't say one way or the other," the lawman growled and sat down with his back to them.

Outside the sheriff's office, they talked softly. Ginger wrinkled her brow, trying to remember something.

"It seems to me there's a thirty day time limit to register the sale of a property with the county clerk. If there's anything sneaky or underhanded about this sale, you can be sure the change in ownership won't be filed before the deadline."

"Let's talk to the county clerk anyway," Buckskin said. "He's probably over being mad at me by now. He might even have found some irregularities in the tax records on the Nelson Ranch."

Maynard Rogers frowned when Buckskin and Ginger walked into his small office. He smiled at Ginger and nodded.

"Morning, Miss Hazleton. What can I do for you today?"

"Those three parcels that went to the sheriff's auction that you told me about a few days ago. Were any of them sold yet?"

"Sheriff said one had sold and the other two would be auctioned off later. He didn't tell me which one it was."

"When was the sale held?"

"Yesterday, near as I know. It wasn't at noon, though, because I was past the steps three times at midday and there weren't no sale done."

"As soon as the papers are filed, I'd like to look at them, Maynard. Will that be all right?"

"You bet, Miss Hazleton. You know about the thirty day waiver period to file the papers?"

"Yes. Oh, Maynard, Mr. Morgan asked about some records on the taxes paid by the Nelsons. Have you had time to check on them yet?"

"No, ma'am, haven't. Get to it this afternoon, if'n I have the time."

"I'd like that, Maynard. It's important. Could be part of a much bigger story. I'd appreciate it."

Maynard nodded.

"Oh, do you know if the tax collector is in? We'd like to have a talk with him."

"Saw him come in this morning. He's just down the hall two doors."

Ginger thanked Rogers, and they moved down the hall to the door marked County Tax Collector. Inside they found a small waiting room cut in half with a two-foot-wide counter. Behind it a bespectacled man with a green eyeshade worked over some ledger books. He glanced up.

"Oh, Miss Hazleton. Nice to see you today. I'm afraid I don't have much news for you this week."

"You might at that, Phineas. This is Buckskin Morgan. He's helping me out at the paper for a while. What type of records do you keep on tax payments?"

"None at all, Miss Hazleton. All payments come through here but the county clerk's staff make the records. All I do is look over the payments, check them against the amount owed and send a list of those paid to the county clerk. I also double-check with the clerk for those not in compliance."

"You ever have any trouble collecting from James Nelson, a small rancher out east of San Carlos Wells?"

"Jim? Never a bit. He always brought in the money a day before the due date. Never missed a payment in the four years he's been out there. I remember 'cause we have a little bet that he wouldn't make a go of the place."

"You won, Phineas. The Something Smith gang shot James Nelson dead about two weeks ago."

"No."

"Afraid so. Also the sheriff sold the Nelson ranch yesterday on a tax sale. Don't you have to turn over a list to the sheriff?"

"Damn right I do! I sent him a list of two places about a week ago. The Nelson ranch wasn't on it." Phineas scowled. He pounded his fist on the counter. "Not the first time the sheriff has tried something like this."

"We checked the records in the county clerk's office, and the Nelson place does not show payments made for the past three years."

"I'll look into that myself. Something damn strange here. Damn strange. Pardon my cursing, Miss Hazleton, but I don't like this happening in my department."

"I've never known you to do anything wrong, Phineas. Let me know what you find out."

Outside on the boardwalk, Buckskin and Ginger conferred again.

"I think it's about time I go and visit the judge," Buckskin said. "Just a quick talk. Then I can evaluate him, check his honesty scale, see if I can rile him up. Might be worth a try."

"But if he is the judge who sets Something Smith loose to torture and kill, won't it be dangerous for you to be up there?"

"Not the least. Up there, you said?"

"His office is on the second floor over the hardware store. He owns the store as well. Get to it by steps up the side of the hardware, or by other stairs in the back, I've heard. Can I come with you?"

"Not this time. I need to do this one alone."

Five minutes later, Buckskin Morgan took the handle of the door that led to the Percival Laudenhimer Enterprises office and thrust open the door. The office was well-appointed with a carpet on the floor and a big desk facing the door. The man who sat there glared up at Buckskin who remained framed in the light of the doorway.

"Who the hell are you and what do you want?" Laudenhimer bellowed. "Come in out of the damn light so I can see you."

"You sure you want to see me, Laudenhimer? You sent at least four men to kill me. What I'm hoping is that you make a play for one of your hideouts."

Buckskin stepped to the side and swung the door closed but kept his right hand near his hogleg.

"You!" Laudenhimer yelped. "What the hell you doing here?"

"Came to see how your little plan is going. First James Nelson gets murdered and his wife raped and scared almost to San Francisco. Then the Nelson ranch taxes aren't paid and the land gets sold at a sheriff's auction. Looks to me like you got a bucketful of explaining to do."

Laudenhimer called out sharply. "Tex, get in here."

"Tex won't be coming, if he's the hombre who tried to shoot me last night. He's down at the undertaker. I'd say you have more than a little explaining to do right about now."

Buckskin drew his six-gun so fast that Laudenhimer's eyes widened and he pushed back from the desk.

"Now hold on, whoever you are, mister. I never laid eyes on you before, don't know your name, don't know nothing about no James Nelson or his ranch. You best put away that iron before it gets you into some real trouble."

"Wouldn't count on it. Leastwise not until I've had my say. It goes like this. Your little land grab won't work. The Nelson taxes were paid, and Mrs. Nelson has legal receipts for each of the past three years. The sheriff's tax sale won't hold up a minute. The county clerk is clearing that up right now.

"That was your big mistake, Laudenhimer. You got too greedy too fast. I'm not sure why yet, but I'm working on it, and I can guarantee that you'll be hearing from me again soon."

Buckskin's .45 aim never left the man's belly. He motioned toward the other door into the room. "You think Tex is coming? Maybe I should go look for him. Maybe I should look for Something Smith, but then he wouldn't know what to do in a fair fight.

"Willy Pointer won't help you any more. Neither will a gent named Larson now six feet under in San Carlos Wells. Looks like you're on your own, Laudenhimer. Let me know what you decide."

Buckskin backed over to the door, made sure no one was behind him, then fired one round into the wall, a foot from where Laudenhimer sat in his chair. The sound echoed around the small room, temporarily deafening both men.

Buckskin waved, cocked the weapon again and eased out the door. He closed it and slid his smoking gun back in leather. On his way down the steps he met two men rushing upward.

"Thought we heard a shot up here," one of the men said.

Buckskin shook his head and pointed to his ears telling them that he couldn't hear what they said. He grinned, continued on down the steps and hurried back to the hotel to see how Sara Jane was.

Chapter Thirteen

It was nearly noon when Buckskin Morgan walked up to his room in the Salt River Hotel. He turned the key gently in the lock and eased the door open an inch so he could see inside.

Sara Jane sat on the bed with her .38 six-gun leveled at the doorway.

"Hey, Buckskin here, don't shoot," he said and pushed the door open so she could see him.

Sara Jane took a long breath and let the weapon down to her lap.

"Glad it's you. I've been wondering what to do. I feel almost back to normal. Tell me what you found out."

He filled her in on everything that had happened that she didn't know about.

"Right now I'm hungry. I'd say that's a good sign. Can I buy you lunch?"

They ate in a small café across the street for a change of pace and talked about the killers.

"Somebody is trying to get my ranch, but we don't know who and we don't know why," Sara Jane said. "That seems to be about it so far."

"They don't want to just get it. They went so far as murder and changing official county records. There must be a lot at stake."

Sara Jane took a spoonful of her soup. "I just don't see what's so valuable on the ranch. It's just a hundred and eighty acres of marginal grazing land and a few buildings."

"Must be something else," Buckskin said. "Railroad going through there or a gold mine. Something has the judge all excited."

"We still don't know for sure who he is?"

"Not for sure, but Percival Laudenhimer is our best bet so far. Right after we eat, we're going over to see Ginger Hazleton at the newspaper and see how she's coming sobering up the old prospector who was suddenly rich and then just as quickly down and out and begging drinks."

"How can he help?

"Not sure, but we have to consider every possible angle here. Anything that happens in this town could be important and have some bearing on our problem."

They finished eating and walked down to the newspaper office. Ginger was at work over a proof. She looked up when they came in and waved.

"Just a minute. Let me finish proofing this page and we can talk."

They waited a short time until Ginger found a stopping place, marked the proof and came up to the slender counter between the front door and the office.

"Last I looked Try Again was still sleeping. Let's go check on him again."

The bunk was empty. Ginger frowned, then they heard sounds in her apartment above and hurried up the steps. Try Again sat at the kitchen table, spreading chunks of bread with jam and butter and finishing off a big glass of milk. He looked up, guilt spread all over his face.

"Oh, damn, I did it again. I was just so hungry. Coming off a drunk I always eat like a horse."

"Don't bother about it. I'm glad you're feeling better," Ginger said. She sat in a chair across the table from him. "You *are* feeling better?"

Try Again beamed. "Couldn't be more chipper. Soon as I get cleaned up a little more, I aim to go out on the street and try to find me a new grubstake. Hey, Miss Ginger, maybe you'd want to do the honors this time. Still got my mule and most of my gear. All I'd need is about thirty dollars worth of good desert food to last me for two months and I'd be out looking to make us both rich."

"Can you remember what happened yesterday?" Ginger asked.

Try Again snorted. "Hell, missie, I was just drunk, not feebleminded. I might be sixty, but I ain't lost my mind yet."

"So you made a good strike—gold or silver?" Buckskin asked.

"Silver, dang you. Best vein of silver I ever saw thrust up that way, just beautiful. I dug around some so I'd know it was the real thing. Went down about three feet and that vein of silver ore just kept going down, down, down. Worth a cotton-picking fortune or I ain't Try Again."

"What did you do then?" Buckskin asked.

"Do? I came straight back here and reported my find to my grubstake partner. He had a right to know. That was almost a month ago now. He told me to rest up and take it easy and to be ready to help him open the mine. Said there was a few things he had to clear up first.

"I rested up, had me a hotel for a while, got some more money off him. Then took that Smith guy out to check out the find. He whooped like all blazes when he saw the strike. Said he'd never seen one richer. We come back and he told my partner it was the real thing.

"Week or so later, my partner gave me two hundred dollars in double eagles. Most money I ever had at one time. That was about two days ago. I spent it like it was water. Yes sirree. Did I have a time. Then I signed a paper with my partner sealing the deal.

"Then something changed. Last night my partner kicked me around his office, took all the money I had left and told me I didn't get no more. I said we had a deal, fifty-fifty on the silver mine. He said I signed a paper giving him all rights to the mine. He tricked me. The son-of-a . . ." He stopped, looked at the two ladies and scowled. "He tricked me."

"The man is a criminal, Try Again. He's a killer and a swindler. We'll see him in jail before this is over. Now, you tell us who your partner is so we can get this all down on paper and make it legal."

"But he's still my partner. Don't know as how I could tell you who he is. We had a solemn oath never to tell. Now I don't know."

Buckskin knelt down beside the table and smiled at the old prospector. "This partner, whoever he is, canceled out your partnership agreement when he cheated you. There is no more solemn oath in force here, Try Again. He cheated you, and now you have no reason to protect him."

"Still seems like I got this agreement with him. Have to think about that some."

"You can tell us where the strike is, since he swindled you out of your half," Ginger said, smiling at the old man.

"Yep, could, but how I know you wouldn't try to get it for yourself? Not meaning you folks, just most folks. A silver strike like this comes along once in a man's life. Still think I own half of it."

He scowled for a minute, then tears filled his eyes and ran over down his cheeks.

"Lordy, I hear that they killed him, that nice gent near where I found the silver. The judge promised me that nothing would happen to the family there, but they murdered him. I figured he should get a third of the silver, but my partner said not a chance. It was fifty-fifty for him and me and nothing for the landowner. Damn it, I should have known they would kill him. He was in their way. The bloody bastards!"

Ginger looked at Buckskin who nodded. "Who killed the man, Try Again?"

"The damn Something Smith gang. Never liked that bunch. Smith did it, or that sneaky one, Willy Pointer."

Sara Jane held on to the table, her face almost white. Buckskin stood and put his arm around her shoulders. He could feel her shivering.

"Who did the Something Smith Gang kill, Try Again," Ginger asked gently.

"Who? The man who owns the ranch, that nice gent, Jim Nelson."

Sara Jane collapsed against Buckskin. He held her a moment, then eased her into a chair. Try Again went on, not noticing Sara Jane's anguish.

"I liked the man. He let me spend a night in the barn now and then. Said not to let on to his wife that I was there. Said she'd worry or want to bring me in the house and give me a bath and make new clothes for me and feed me. I was happy the way I was. I never told Jim about finding the silver on his land. Figured my partner would do that."

Try Again sobbed a moment, then wiped his eyes. "Dang, they killed him. Heard Something Smith talking about it once in the office up there. Damn him!"

"Was your partner in your grubstake the same man who told Something Smith and his gang to kill Jim Nelson?" Ginger asked, her voice low and soft.

Try Again brightened. "Oh, sure, thought I told you that. The judge told them to kill him. I heard him one day I was up there in his office. The judge grubstaked me three years when nobody else in town would. I figure I owed him for all the cash he put out for me."

The rear door to the newspaper plant opened and then closed with a soft rattle.

"Somebody came in the back door," Ginger whispered. Buckskin signaled for them all to be quiet and tiptoed to the head of the stairs that led up to the kitchen. The three came out so they could see what was happening.

Sara Jane pulled the .38 revolver from her purse and held it ready. She thumbed back the hammer and waited.

One of the steps squeaked, and Buckskin knelt down, waiting. Another step sounded as weight went on it. Buckskin turned and saw the three not ten feet behind him and in the line of fire. He motioned them back. The two women moved back a step and waited, but Try Again stood there watching.

The first shot caught them all by surprise. It careened off the top step and slapped into the roof. Buckskin fell flat on the floor and fired three times. The gunman below fired twice more. When Sara Jane shot her .38 once, Buckskin saw a shape below and fired again. A scream knifed through the echoing shots in the closed space.

Buckskin charged down the steps.

"Easy, don't move," he growled. "Keep your damn hand away from that hogleg or you're dead meat, understand?"

A scream rang out upstairs. Buckskin grabbed the wounded bushwhacker and dragged him up the six steps to the top. He saw Ginger kneeling beside Try Again.

Buckskin pulled the wounded man over to the edge of the living room where Try Again lay. Buckskin knew at once what had happened. Try Again had taken a round in the forehead. There was no chance he could live through a wound like that. He knelt beside the body and checked it for breath and pulse, finding neither.

"I'm sorry," he said, "but we have his killer." Buckskin searched the killer, took away a hideout and a knife, then tied his hands behind his back and his ankles together.

Buckskin slapped his face hard enough to jolt his head to the other side. "Who hired you to kill me?" he asked so softly the man could barely hear.

The man snorted but remained silent.

Sara Jane dropped to her knees beside the man on the floor and slammed the butt of her .38 into the killer's wounded shoulder. He bleated in pain.

"You know I can't tell you," he hissed through clenched teeth, trying to hold in the pain.

"You better," Sara Jane said. "Probably the same man who ordered my husband killed." Sara Jane set her jaw, closed her eyes to slits and hit the man's wounded shoulder twice with her .38. He bellowed in pain and rolled over, hate glinting from his eyes.

He could barely speak. The words came out softly, yet distinctly. "Damn you, it was the judge. A man who is called the judge hired me."

Buckskin grunted. "Ginger, you have a place downstairs we can stash this garbage for a few days?"

She nodded, brought a clean dish towel, tore it into strips and bandaged the man's arm so it wouldn't bleed any more.

When she was done Buckskin hoisted the man over his shoulder like a sack of wheat and carried him downstairs to a room just off the back door. It was six feet square and had a door with a hasp on the outside. Buckskin cut loose the killer's feet and lay him on the floor.

"Don't go anywhere. If you're lucky they'll hang you quick for killing Try Again, the prospector."

Buckskin closed the door, put the hasp on and pushed a nail through it, locking the killer inside. Back upstairs, Ginger had Sara Jane sitting in the kitchen chair. She had taken out a bottle of brandy, and Sara Jane was sipping at the drink from a glass.

"I . . . I don't know how I get so angry. When I see one of these animals who kill, I just want to wipe them off the face of the earth. One of them killed my James." She was close to tears. She sniffed and wiped her eyes, then stood up.

"All right, I'm ready. What is there to be done next?"

Buckskin carried Try Again's body down to the back door. "We'll tell the sheriff about this at the right time," he said. "First I want to have another talk with the judge. We might be able to wrap this up here without even going out to the ranch."

"I want to go with you," Sara Jane said. "It was my James who this judge had killed."

Ginger shook her head. Buckskin caught Sara Jane in his arms and held her in a tight embrace.

"Sara Jane, you've done beautifully in your pledge to do away with James' three killers. But this time it's my turn to go and confront the judge. We can't risk you getting hurt at this late date. This vengeance ride is almost over for you. I want you to promise to stay here with Ginger until I get back. Agreed?"

Sara Jane eased back from him and nodded slowly.

"Yes, but I still have one more killer to go—two if we count the judge. Promise that you'll leave them for me to deal with."

Buckskin said he would, not knowing if he could keep that kind of a promise or not. He ran out the back door and down the alley, heading for the judge's office and a showdown.

Chapter Fourteen

It had at last all fallen into place. The so-called judge, Percival Laudenhimer, had stumbled onto a rich silver strike through the old prospector and wanted it all to himself. He made sure the strike was really there, then had Something Smith kill James Nelson who lived on the land, changed the tax records and had the ranch put up for a sheriff's sale.

He probably was the only bidder for the rigged sale with the sheriff, but such a sale could be countermanded by the county clerk and tax collector.

Now the target was Laudenhimer. He must be a man who was never satisfied with what he had.

Buckskin came around the corner from the alley in back of the newspaper office to Main Street and saw a puff of smoke across the street. At the same time something hit him in the left shoulder, and he cried out in pain as he fell backwards into the alley. He rolled to the left in back of the brick bank building and pulled his six-gun.

Another damned bushwhacker. Wait him out. The bastard would come check on his kill. Buckskin's left arm throbbed like it was full of Fourth of July rockets. He tried to see the wound but couldn't.

He had to keep his attention to the front. A shadow appeared at the mouth of the alley from the afternoon sun but it passed on by—just someone walking across the alley, he guessed. Buckskin didn't move. He lay still enough for a man to consider him sleeping or dead. Only his eyes moved.

Another shadow slanted across the open alley and stopped by the far wall. Buckskin looked that way but couldn't see clearly without moving his head. That he couldn't do. He waited.

The shadow moved again across the alley mouth toward the side where he lay. Now he saw the man, tall with white hair escaping from his dark hat. He concentrated on the face—yes, Something Smith.

Buckskin had placed his six-gun in front of him, head on his arm, finger in the trigger. Now he shifted the muzzle, jolted upright to his knees and caught Something Smith with his weapon down. The gunman brought it up to point and shoot, but Buckskin fired first. The upward angle and his quick shot pulled his aim off, and instead of taking the man in the chest, the round pulled to the right and hit the killer in his left shoulder, spinning him backward.

Something Smith's own round thundered just after Buckskin's, but it hit the side of the bank's bricks and ricocheted down the alley.

Smith turned and ran with Buckskin in pursuit. The street was nearly empty in midafternoon, but there were still too many for Buckskin to take a chance shooting. Something Smith had no such morals. He turned, fired twice and missed. Three shots from Smith, Buckskin counted. He still had four, his enemy two.

Smith charged past a team of six, around it to the back, then darted across the street, using a woman driving a light buggy as his cover.

Buckskin raced ahead, not bothering about his bleeding arm. He angled across the street to shorten the distance. Smith could run. He gained distance between them by the time he hit the next alley.

Buckskin had to hold up to be sure that Something Smith wasn't just around the end of the alley waiting for him. He wasn't.

Buckskin saw Smith round the corner and head toward a pair of houses on the far side of the next street. One of the houses had a red light hanging over the front door. It was a symbol that some of the sporting houses had started to use to advertise their business.

Something Smith charged through the door of the sporting house without stopping. It was an advantage to him. He could get a quick shot through a window at his pursuer as he charged up. Buckskin shifted his course and came up on the near side of the place, then ran around to the front and through the opening without a stop, holding his six-gun ready as he ran.

Inside the bawdy house's front door was a small entryway with doors opening to the left into a parlor where some of the girls waited for business. The other door was closed, and straight ahead was a stairway.

Before he could more than shout, a woman came out of the parlor dressed in a robe that had lost its belt and gaped open from her throat to her toes. She yelled at Buckskin and swung a broom at him, grazing his side.

Another woman ran down the stairs, a mop handle in her hands, brandishing it like a sword. Two more women appeared behind her, one with a hammer, another with a big wrench.

Buckskin stopped and laughed. "What the hell you ladies think you're doing, protecting a client? That bastard who just ran in here put a bullet in my shoulder. He's a damned bushwhacker. He also killed at least one man in the past two weeks. That the kind of men you want for customers?"

"He pays his money, we don't ask questions," the woman with the broom spat. "Now get the hell out of here."

Buckskin laughed and lifted his .45. He put two more rounds in the empty chambers, making six. The women watched him. One had her mouth open, and two were about ready to run. He figured the place didn't have a basement, so he swung the Colt toward the floor and fired a shot through the pine planking.

Three of the women ran, looking back with frightened faces. The one with the broom gripped her weapon harder. The mop handle whore on the stairs took two steps up and stopped.

"Oh, hell, I might as well shoot one of you to show you that I mean business." He brought up the Colt and aimed at the woman on the stairs. She dropped the mop handle and scurried up the steps.

Buckskin ran up right after her but stopped when his line of sight let him peer over the floor boards. A six-gun snarled ahead of him and wood chipped out of the top step as the round narrowly missed him.

Buckskin snapped a shot off down the hall at the half-open door where the blush of white smoke gave away the shooter. The door shut, and Buckskin could hear a key turn in the lock.

Buckskin figured the distance to the ground. Hanging out a second story window it was about a five foot drop. Not enough to worry about. He stepped to the second floor and darted across the hall into the first room. A naked woman and a man lay on the bed, both panting in the afterglow.

"Sorry," he said and hurried to the window. He lifted it as quietly as he could and looked out. Something Smith had lost his hat. His white hair was mussed as he hung by his hands on the edge of the window sill.

Buckskin knew he should kill him, but he aimed at the big man's right shoulder and fired. The round pulled a little, slammed into Something Smith's right shoulder and knocked him off the window. He dropped to the ground, rolled and fired once at the window. Buckskin quickly ducked below.

One more round came through the opening, then Buckskin went out the window, hung and dropped before the other man had a chance to reload and fire. Something Smith must have realized his dilemma, because as soon as Buckskin came though the window, he stood and ran down the alley in back of the houses.

It wasn't a real alley, just an open space behind the houses. Beyond that there was nothing but open country with a few cactus and some sage.

Buckskin hit the ground, rolled and felt his ankle go. He stood and limped. Not a chance he was going to catch Something Smith now. He had hit a rock with one boot and had twisted his ankle. He limped another ten feet down the alley, then turned and headed for town.

He had an appointment with the judge, and his time was fast running out.

Five minutes later, Buckskin hobbled up the steps and looked in the judge's front office window. Nobody seemed to be there. It was late afternoon, but there was no lamp burning inside. He knocked but got no response. Buckskin used his good right foot and kicked the door right beside the doorknob.

The door flew open, and he walked inside. Nobody home. Buckskin lit a nearby lamp and checked the merchant's desk. He found no maps, no lists, nothing incriminating. Neither did he find a bill of sale for the Nelson ranch from the county sheriff.

It was time for a short chat with that lawman. Buckskin blew out the lamp, closed the front door and walked to the sheriff's office. The more he walked on the ankle the better it felt. It wasn't a serious sprain, just some stretched muscles. He'd never know it happened if he kept moving.

Sheriff Abady was in his office. Buckskin waved at the one deputy on duty and walked into the lawman's quarters.

"Evening, Sheriff. You and I have a lot of talking to do, so we better get right at it."

"I got nothing to say to you. I'd appreciate it if you left my office right now."

"Not possible until I have my say. The problem is, Sheriff, you're up to your tin badge in an illegal conspiracy to defraud that has now extended to a double murder, and it all can come and sit right on your doorstep."

Buckskin watched him a minute, then went on. "Seeing how you don't want to confess and throw yourself on the mercy of the court, I'll spell it out for you.

"Try Again found a silver mine. He told Percival Laudenhimer, who promptly checked out the find. When he knew the strike was rich, he ordered the owner of the land, James Nelson, killed. That done, he changed the payment records of taxes on the property, then told you to hold a legal land sale to reclaim taxes owed the county.

"You did, and Percival Laudenhimer was the only bidder. Then Laudenhimer dumped the prospector, Try Again, who promptly got drunk and told everything he knew to the one friend he had in town, Miss Ginger Hazleton.

"You saw the problem and hired a fiddlefoot cowboy to murder the prospector and shut him up. The cowboy did so, but we captured him and are now holding him for trial. We have three eyewitnesses. The man's as good as hung, but he'll take you with him since you hired him."

Sheriff Abady held up both hands. "No, I didn't hire him. Laudenhimer did. Said Try Again was too dangerous with his blabbing and then he . . ." The sheriff stopped, a look of anger and dismay shrouding his face.

"Sheriff, I know the territorial attorney general over at the capitol. Do you want me to go get him right now, or will you toe the line and I'll see what I can do about getting the conspiracy to change tax records cleared up for you?"

Abady rubbed his hands over his face. He was sweating like a horse after a mile gallop. "Look, it was all Laudenhimer's doing. He said he'd give me an election campaign contribution if I had the land sale at night with nobody else there. I didn't touch the tax records. Laudenhimer did it all. I even got a legal order from the county tax collector to take over those properties. Don't know as I did anything illegal.

"But I'll toe the line. You bet. I'll pick up that killer. Laudenhimer must have sent him. I didn't."

Buckskin stood. The sheriff was still sweating like a whore on a busy Saturday night.

"You go down to the newspaper office. Tell Ginger I talked with you and you're there to pick up the killer and jail him. You have papers on him before morning charging him with murder, you understand?"

"Yes, sir, I do. Wasn't nobody supposed to be killed."

"There never is, Sheriff. Never is."

Outside the courthouse, Buckskin looked at his Waterbury. Time to get to the newspaper and back to the county clerk's office before he closed.

He told Ginger the sheriff would be coming to pick up the killer. "I had a heart-to-heart talk with him. He'll play the game straight now or hang."

Ginger and Sara Jane fussed over his wounded shoulder. They made him take off his shirt and found that the bullet had gone all the way through. They doctored the wound, then tied a good tight bandage around it to stop any more bleeding. Then he and Sara Jane left for the county clerk's office.

They just made it before he closed. Buckskin pointed to Sara Jane. "Mr. Rogers, I don't believe you know Mrs. James Nelson. She's here to check on the mistake in your records about her payment of the taxes on the Nelson ranch over the other side of San Carlos Wells."

Maynard Rogers was all smiles. "Mrs. Nelson, I'm sorry to hear about the loss of your husband. My condolences. I do have good news, though. The error in your records has been found. It wasn't an error, really. Someone had done a poor job of trying to blot out the payment notations on your property.

"That has all been rectified. The property is paid up to date, and the illegal notification to the sheriff for the sale has been corrected. The illegal sale of the property by the sheriff is null and void, so you have nothing at all to worry about."

Outside the clerk's office, Sara Jane reached up and kissed Buckskin on the cheek. "I'll offer even better thanks when we're in a more private situation," she said with a glint in her eye. "Now, what's next? We still haven't found Something Smith and the judge."

"I figure we just missed both of them. My hunch is that they're on the five o'clock stage I saw pulling out from the depot not a half hour ago.

"Way I hear it, there's another one through here about eight o'clock in the morning. We couldn't beat the judge to San Carlos Wells even if we rode all night. I suggest we rest up here tonight, have a nice supper, and be on that stage in the morning."

"I was about to suggest the same thing. But what can we do all evening after supper?"

"If you don't know, I have a couple of ideas," Buckskin said.

Buckskin couldn't remember a more delightful meal. They at last got to sleep sometime after midnight and made the stage the next morning without breakfast and not five minutes to spare.

After ten hours of bouncing and jolting and with stops every ten miles to change horses at the swing stations, Buckskin and Sara Jane arrived in San Carlos Wells, tired and hungry and anxious for some good food and then a soft bed.

They would head out for the ranch the next morning, but first they needed a good night's sleep. They ate at the hotel, then sat on the bed in their room and stared at each other.

Sara Jane reached over and pecked a quick kiss on his cheek. "Buckskin Morgan, you're the best man I've ever been to bed with, but tonight I'm just simply too tired to poke."

"Good, that makes two of us. Let's get some sleep."

The next morning at breakfast, they made their final plans. They rented horses from the livery and rode to the general store.

"I've got a lot of staples at the ranch, but there are some things we'll need," Sara Jane explained. "I figure it might take us two or three days to find the strike. Remember, Try Again said he had dug down three feet or so to be sure. It gives us something to look for."

They bought bacon, a ham and two steaks to roast over the fire as soon as they got to the ranch house.

"I hope it's still there," Sara Jane said. "You don't suppose anyone has burned down the ranch house, do you?"

They rode out from San Carlos Wells just after eight o'clock and had their first sighting of the ranch buildings just after noon. Everything looked as it was when they had left the place over a week and a half ago.

Buckskin had just set a fire with kindling and some crumpled paper in the stove and was about to light it when he blew out the match.

"No fire," he said.

Sara Jane looked at him as if he'd lost his mind. "What in the world do you mean, no fire? How can we fry those steaks without a fire?"

"We can't, and we shouldn't. We figure that both Something Smith and the judge are out here somewhere looking for the mine. At least one of them must have a map that Try Again made for them. Something Smith's even been to the spot before with the old prospector. What do you think they'll do if they are already on the ranch and see smoke coming from the chimney?"

Sara Jane nodded. "You're right. What we should be doing is watching to see if we can spot any sign of them. Come on, I have just the place. It's not a quarter of a mile away but you can see for five miles in all but one direction. Let's each get a rifle and go take a good look for them."

Chapter Fifteen

Before they left the cabin, they had a cold lunch of ham sandwiches and water from the inside pump. They put their horses in a shed so nobody could see them. Then they walked up a narrow rise behind the house. The slope continued into a ridge that swept eastward for two miles into the higher ground of the hills.

They stopped about a quarter of a mile from the house near some wood and Sara Jane pointed.

"We can see to the north all the way past our property line, then to the west almost into San Carlos Wells, and again to the south beyond our property."

Buckskin concentrated on the area to the west. He tried to figure the time. Chances were that both men caught the evening stage, which would put them into town yesterday about four A.M. A night ride on a stagecoach was worse than doing time in the territorial prison.

160

"My guess is that the judge got in late the night before last and took to a bed in the hotel. He probably didn't get up until at least noon so he isn't more than about eight hours of daylight ahead of us."

"Think he came out here to look for the strike?"

"He has to. He has a map I'd bet the ranch on, and Something Smith must be with him. He wouldn't travel out here without some protection."

"Which means they came looking yesterday about noon and should be at the strike and have made a camp."

"My guess."

"Then why don't we see any smoke?"

"I'm no expert in silver mining, but most of the claims and strikes I've seen have been in ridge country with lots of geological breaks and upthrusts, sheets of rock and strata showing. Not likely there's gonna be a silver strike anywhere down on the gentle, rolling plateau or valley."

"Let's give it another half hour. We might see a dust trail or a rider or something. The judge might have sent Something Smith into town for supplies or such."

They waited, but nothing happened.

"Time to get the horses and investigate that quarter of your ranch we can't see, the part up in the breaks and ridges."

They went back to the ranch, walked out the horses, then mounted and rode. Both had rifles in saddle boots and six-guns on their hips. Buckskin led the way up the ridge. When he could see some of the breaks and hogbacks and gullies ahead and to the right, he reined in and they scanned the area closely.

Buckskin had learned how to check out an area when he worked with an old Army scout. You divided the space into sections and worked each section slowly and carefully, appraising each suspicious area with a critical eye.

If nothing developed, you moved on to the next section. When all the parts of the area had been worked closely, you scanned the whole thing for any sudden movement or change in appearance.

He found nothing in this section.

They rode again. This time they had to drop down along the side of the surging ridge they were on that rose to a mountain in the distance. They slipped along the side of the ridge and found two more canyons to check. Nothing.

By three that afternoon, they had looked over more than a dozen arroyos and their ridges but found not a single rider.

"We're off our property," Sara Jane said. "This is part of our grazing range, but we don't own it. We have to swing to the north now and angle back to the west."

They rode for a half hour and then came to a ridge they hadn't seen before. Buckskin rode up to the lip of the land mass and at once backed his horse down.

"Paydirt," he said. He dismounted, and Sara Jane slid off her horse as well.

"What did you see?" She didn't wait to find out but scrambled up to the ridge line and looked over. Below she saw a narrow arroyo. On the far side a small tent had been set up with a fire burning in front of it. Nearby on the side of the ridge they could see an upthrust of rock. It formed a strata line extending along the side of the ridge for 50 feet, then vanished underground.

A man with his shirt off worked with a shovel near the far end of the upthrust, a weathered and evidently tough slab of upright rock strata.

"That's it," Buckskin said softly. "The Nelson silver mine. Not much yet, but it should make you a wealthy lady."

"A strike, a mine," Sara Jane said. "Do I own the mineral rights on this land? I don't know about Arizona territorial law. Since this is my property, do I have to file a claim on it like I was on government property?"

Buckskin grinned. "Those are questions we'll get answered over at the territorial capital after we take care of those claim jumpers."

"Only one man is down there. If the judge is there he wouldn't be using the shovel. So where is he?"

Buckskin nodded. "I been worried about that. Only one horse down there that I can see."

"So what now?" Sara Jane asked.

"I'm going down and take Smith. If I get pinned down, you use that rifle and scare whoever has me under his gun. You don't have to hit anyone. Just scare them, and I'll be able to move again."

"I can do that." Sara Jane frowned. "You be careful. I don't want to lose you at this late date."

"I have no intention of getting shot again. This one left arm with two bullet holes in it is enough for one week."

Buckskin went over the lip of the ridge behind a line of sagebrush. He worked slowly, his six-gun tied down with the strap and his Spencer rifle dragging its stock in the dirt as he crawled on hands and knees.

The sides of the arroyo were not bare, but from a distance they looked that way. Buckskin found waist-high sage here and there and a little bit of chaparral to hide behind. When the man below turned his back and shoveled dirt into a pile, Buckskin rose and ran a dozen yards before he dropped back to a bit of cover.

It was slow going. He had over 80 yards to cover before he would be close enough to yell at the man and put him under his rifle at close range. The tent still bothered Buckskin. It was no more than six feet square, but was the judge inside it or not?

He surged ahead again and figured he was half-way there. The sides of the canyon came down sharply just ahead, and he was afraid of sliding down and making noise. He checked the steep area which was not over ten feet wide, ending in the sandy bottom where runoff water from sudden desert cloudbursts had left a soft deposit.

Buckskin waited until the man below turned his back, then Buckskin jumped. He landed hard, bent his knees to absorb the shock and sprawled flat in the bottom of the gully. At that time he was out of sight of the digger. The rifle fell from his hands and clattered on the rocks.

Buckskin remained flat. He was sure the shoveler had heard the rifle fall. He turned, brought up his six-gun and waited. Two or three minutes later he heard boots on gravel coming toward him. The moment he saw a head over the lip of rock above him, Buckskin stood up, his weapon cocked and centered on Something Smith's belly.

"We meet again, Smith. Ease that hogleg out of your hand and drop it on the ground. Now!"

Smith's eyes went wide in shock and anger. He trembled, and for a moment Buckskin thought the killer would lift the weapon from where it pointed at his feet. Then Smith shrugged and dropped the six-gun.

"Been waiting for you to show up. Took you long enough."

"We wanted to give you enough hemp to get yourself dropped through the trapdoor back in Phoenix. Where's the judge?"

"Who?"

"Percival Laudenhimer, your boss."

Before Smith could answer a rifle shot blasted into the still Arizona desert and Smith spun, taking a round in the left leg. He jolted to the ground and rolled into the bottom of the arroyo.

"What the hell?"

Buckskin shrugged. "That's the woman you raped in her own bed, the one whose husband you murdered. You remember her—Sara Jane Nelson."

Buckskin stood and looked back at the ridge where a small puff of white smoke showed Sara Jane's position. "No," Buckskin bellowed at the widow. "Don't shoot." He turned back to Smith, lifted him and pushed him toward the tent.

"Where's the judge?"

"Ain't here."

"Good, you can take the rap for murder and claim jumping all by yourself."

"I didn't kill Nelson. Willy Pointer did."

"You were there, you had the assignment. Doesn't matter who pulled the trigger. You'll hang just the same."

"Ain't right."

"Neither is it right you raping her and bushwhacking me twice—or was it three times?"

Buckskin tied Smith's hands behind him.

"If you don't mind, I'm going to clear that tent just to make sure the judge isn't having a nap while you dig the claim for him."

"Don't bother." A heavy voice sounded from near the tent behind Buckskin. He looked up to see the twin muzzles of a shotgun aimed at him from not more than 20 feet. Percival Laudenhimer held the weapon and grinned.

"Interesting what you hear when nobody knows you're around. Now I'd say that you, Mr. Morgan, have just interfered with my plans for the last time."

Buckskin recognized the twitch in the man's face. He was going to shoot. Buckskin saw the judge's finger tightening on the trigger. He jolted to the left, grabbing Something Smith as a shield.

Both barrels of the shotgun blasted at the same time, and Buckskin felt and smelled some of the double aught buck slamming past him. There were 13 of the slugs in each shell, and all 26 came slamming at him and Something Smith at killing speed.

Buckskin felt Something Smith blasted back against him, and at the same time something cut through his left leg and pounded into the heel of his left boot.

Then Buckskin was flat on his back with Something Smith over him. Buckskin had reached for his iron just before the scattergun fired, and now he completed the draw and sent one round at the small man in his usual black suit and vest.

From the ridge he heard a rifle fire twice, then three times, and the Judge went down screaming in anger and agony.

Buckskin pushed Something Smith off him and surged to his feet. He ran to where the judge lay on his side. The shotgun had fallen to the left out of reach. Percival Laudenhimer screamed in pain and held his shoulder and his left leg. Blood poured from both wounds.

Buckskin looked back at Something Smith. No problem there. Two of the big slugs from the shotgun had caught the outlaw in the face and had penetrated his brain.

"Easy, Laudenhimer. You aren't hurt that bad. You're lucky one of those rifle slugs didn't go through your belly. Then you'd know what real pain is."

Buckskin saw Sara Jane lead the horses over the lip of the ridge and work down the slope.

"It's all over now. I'll just wrap up those wounds so you can live to hang. I'm charging you with the murder of Something Smith. Can't say it's much of a loss to the community, but it's enough to put a strong hemp rope around your neck. Now stop the bellowing and take your pain like a man. You tried for too much, and you'll wind up hung by the neck until you are dead, dead, dead."

Buckskin tied up the wounds with the tail of the judge's shirt, then secured his hands behind him.

Buckskin and Sara Jane looked at the mining strike. It was an upthrust of some kind of hard rock, basalt maybe, Buckskin guessed. He had no idea what a silver vein looked like. It was just another rock to him with blue striations in it.

"If Try Again said it was a real silver strike, I believe him," Sara Jane said. "The trouble is, I don't have the slightest idea what to do next."

"Ask around in Phoenix. There are companies that specialize in taking over a claim or a mine and running it on percentages with the owner. It's a good arrangement for both parties. That way you don't have to know anything about mining. You should be able to find one that would pay

you a five thousand dollar advance against your
future profits."

"Oh, my!" Sara Jane said. "I guess I could get
used to that." She looked over at Something Smith
and shuddered. She took a long breath and caught
Buckskin's hand. "At least I didn't have to kill that
one. The judge did it for me. Now we better be
getting back to the ranch house so I can cook us
a proper supper. Even the killer over there needs
some food."

Three days later in Phoenix, they had turned
Laudenhimer over to the sheriff, and the district
attorney swore out a murder warrant against him.
His trial would be within three weeks. Buckskin
gave a deposition as to the murder, and Sara
Jane would testify. Buckskin said the trial itself
shouldn't take more than an hour and a half
including the jury's deliberations.

They sat in a small café across from the hotel
and had just finished supper.

"What will you do now?" Sara Jane asked.

"Figure I'll continue on toward San Francisco.
That's where I was heading when I met you."

"You don't have to go." She looked away, then
turned, took his hand and looked into his eyes
with an open, eager expression. "I want you to
stay here. Stay and keep a watch on the mining
company we hired. They could cheat a woman
alone, and I'd never know it. Stay here and help
me run the ranch. I still want to make it pay off,
just to prove that James was right. I might not
need the money by then, but I want to show James
that he was right and it can pay off."

She sighed and touched his cheek. "Then, too,
I was hoping that you'd stay on and marry me.
Make an honest woman of me and help me raise
two kids and become a part of Arizona's future.

No sense your riding off to who knows what, when you have a rich widow who's willing and who owns a ranch and a silver mine."

Buckskin grinned and held both her hands. "I'd like to, Sara Jane. I really would, but I've still got too much wanderlust in my blood. In six months or a year I'd get a hankering to hit the trail again, and I'd be gone. Wouldn't be fair to you.

"I'm not the settling-down kind—not yet, anyway. Maybe in ten years I'll see it different. Right now I have to be free to ride the trails, to solve those little problems that my customers have. But I'll never forget you."

Sara Jane sighed and nodded grimly as if she had expected his answer. "Could we have one more time? The afternoon stage doesn't leave until two o'clock. We have almost four hours that needn't go to waste."

Buckskin nodded. They hurried across the street and up to their room. One last time, Buckskin Morgan thought, then it was out on the trail. To what? He didn't know, and that was where the thrill of it lay for him. Another adventure waiting to happen. Right then, he nearly couldn't wait to be off on a new case, a new assignment, a new adventure. He was still Buckskin Morgan, still looking for adventure and trouble and interesting women. Yeah!

BUCKSKIN
KIT DALTON

**The hard-riding, hard-bitten
Adult Western series that's hotter'n a
blazing pistol and as tough as the men and
women who tamed the frontier!**

#28: APACHE RIFLES. Working as a scout for the U.S. Army, Lee Morgan tracked the deadly Chircahau Apache—and found a dangerous Indian maid who had eyes for him.
_2943-X $2.95

#29: RETURN FIRE. Searching for a missing prospector in Deadwood, South Dakota, Lee Morgan found the only help anymore would give him was a one-way ticket to boot hill.
_3009-8 $2.95 US/$3.50 CAN

#30: RIMFIRE REVENGE. Escorting a rancher's spoiled wife and voluptuous daughter to their new Colorado home, Morgan found a passel of corpses and arrows enough to start an Indian War.
_3082-9 $2.95 US/$3.95 CAN

 **DIRK FLETCHER**

The pistol-hot Western series filled with more brawls and beauties than a frontier saloon on a Saturday night!

Spur #40: Texas Tramp. When a band of bloodthirsty Comanches kidnaps the sultry daughter of a state senator, the sheriff of Sweet Springs call on Spur McCoy to rescue the tempting Penny Wallington. Once McCoy chops the Indians' totem poles down to size, he will have Penny for his thoughts—and a whole lot of woman in his hands.
_3523-5 $3.99 US/$4.99 CAN

Spur #39: Minetown Mistress. While tracking down a missing colonel in Idaho Territory, Spur runs into a luscious blonde and a randy redhead who appoint themselves his personal greeters. He'll waste no time finding the lost man— because only then can he take a ride with the fillies who drive his private welcome wagon.

_3448-4 $3.99 US/$4.99 CAN

Spur #38: Free Press Filly. Sent to investigate the murder of a small-town newspaper editor, McCoy is surprised to discover his contact is Gypsy, the man's busty daughter, who believes in a free press and free love. Gun's blazing, lust raging, McCoy has to kill the killer so he can put the story— and Gypsy—to bed.
_3394-1 $3.99 US/$4.99 CAN

LEISURE BOOKS
ATTN: Order Department
276 5th Avenue, New York, NY 10001

Please add $1.50 for shipping and handling for the first book and $.35 for each book thereafter. PA., N.Y.S. and N.Y.C. residents, please add appropriate sales tax. No cash, stamps, or C.O.D.s. All orders shipped within 6 weeks via postal service book rate. Canadian orders require $2.00 extra postage and must be paid in U.S. dollars through a U.S. banking facility.

Name _____
Address _____
City _____ State _____ Zip _____
I have enclosed $_____ in payment for the checked book(s).
Payment <u>must</u> accompany all orders.☐ Please send a free catalog.

by Dirk Fletcher

The adult Western series that's got more straight shootin' than a day at the O.K. Corral and more wild lovin' than a night in a frontier cathouse!

#35: Wyoming Wildcat. Missing government surveyors, long-legged hellcats, greedy ranchers, and trigger-happy gunmen—they're all in a day's work for Spur McCoy. But he'll beat down a hundred bushwhackers and still have the strength to tame any wildcat who strays across his path!
_3192-2 $3.50 US/$4.50 CAN

#36: Mountain Madam. In Oregon's Wallowa Mountains, murderous fanatics are executing anyone who stands in the way of their fiendish conspiracy to reap a heavenly reward. But with the help of a tantalizing godsend named Angelina, McCoy will stop the infernal plot.
_3289-9 $3.50 US/$4.50 CAN